Yevge.

Islanders

and The Fisher of Men

Translated by Sophie Fuller and Julian Sacchi

FLAMINGO

Published by Fontana Paperbacks

First published in Russia 1918
First published in this translation by
The Salamander Press 1984

This Flamingo edition first published
in 1985 by Fontana Paperbacks,
8 Grafton Street, London W1X 3LA

Flamingo is an imprint of
Fontana Paperbacks, a division
of the Collins Publishing Group

Made and printed in Great Britain by
William Collins Sons & Co. Ltd, Glasgow

CONTENTS

Introduction, 9
Islanders, 13
The Fisher of Men, 73

INTRODUCTION

Yevgeny Zamyatin was born in the Russian provincial town of Lebedyan in 1884. He studied naval engineering in St Petersburg and as a student was an active member of the Bolshevik party. He was imprisoned and then exiled after the revolution of 1905 but lived illegally in St Petersburg and still managed to graduate. He began to publish his stories in 1908 while working in shipbuilding and lecturing on naval engineering at the Polytechnic Institute.

During the First World War he spent a year and a half in England, supervising the construction of Russian ice-breakers in Glasgow, Sunderland, South Shields and Newcastle-upon-Tyne. He returned to Russia just before the October Revolution in 1917, and remained in Petrograd during the harsh Civil War years.

From the first, his outspoken essays and the 'anti-Soviet ideology' contained in his literary work brought him into ever increasing disfavour with the authorities and the new proletarian writers. In 1920 he wrote his famous dystopian novel *We*. Its bleak portrayal of a rationalist state in the future made publication difficult in the Soviet Union. By 1924 an English translation had appeared in New York, with Zamyatin's consent. The first Russian version was published in a White émigré journal in 1927.

Throughout the twenties, pressure increased on those writers, known as the fellow travellers, who had not wholeheartedly embraced the Revolution and Bolshevik ideas. This culminated in 1929 in an attack on Pilnyak and Zamyatin for publishing ideologically unsound works abroad. Unlike Pilnyak, Zamyatin refused to recant. Further savage attacks followed and it became almost impossible for him to get his work published.

In June 1931 he sent a letter to Stalin asking for permission to leave the Soviet Union, in which he wrote: 'Just as the Christians once invented the devil as a convenient personification of every kind of evil, so the critics have made me the devil of Soviet literature.' Perhaps because Gorky interceded for him, Zamyatin was given permission to go abroad for a year. He never returned to Russia and died of a heart attack in Paris in 1937.

Zamyatin's preoccupations were common to many of the writers of his time. Writers' reactions to the social upheavals caused by emergent industrialisation and two revolutions were expressed in differing ways. The Futurists celebrated the new age of speed and machines; other writers were more concerned that basic human values would be destroyed by the power of the machine. The works of fellow travellers such as Babel, Olesha and Pilnyak in the twenties are permeated with a sense of struggle between the old and the new, the primitive and the civilised, man and machine.

Zamyatin saw the world in terms of an eternal struggle between forces of energy and forces of entropy, found in the established and dogmatic. Entropy lulled man into a dangerous complacency. What fought against entropy was revolution and heretical thought, the energy of an unquenchable life force.

Zamyatin welcomed the October Revolution for its necessary disruption of the old static order, but as time passed he could see that this once vital force was settling into an inflexible entropy. It is easy to see why the Soviet authorities found, and still find, his ideas unacceptable. Zamyatin's call was always for new energy, new revolutions: 'Revolution is everywhere, in everything. It is endless. There is no final revolution, no final number.'

Writing should be a vital part of this energy. And Zamyatin foresaw the danger of literary stagnation: 'True literature can only exist where it is created, not by conscientious and loyal officials, but by madmen, hermits, heretics, dreamers, rebels and sceptics.'

Zamyatin came to England in March 1916: 'Until then, Germany was the only place I had visited in the West. Berlin seemed to be a condensed, eighty per cent version of Petersburg. England was different. Everything there was as new and strange as it had been in Alexandria and Jerusalem. Here at first it was all iron, machines and blueprints.'

Islanders was written here in 1917. The idea of an English gentleman blackmailing lovers he discovered in parks was originally one that Zamyatin had intended to use as the ending of *Islanders*. However, it subsequently became a separate story, *The Fisher of Men*, which he wrote in 1918, after his return to Russia.

Zamyatin was obviously fascinated by England and the English. He wrote several articles on H. G. Wells, whose visions of the future were echoed in Zamyatin's *We*. In its turn, *We* was to influence the most famous English dystopian novel—George Orwell's *1984*.

The regulated, restricted life of the respectable English middle class seemed to Zamyatin to be a perfect example of the horrors of entropy. He depicts a world where everything has its correct place, where the vases displayed in every window on one side of the street are blue and on the other green. It is a world in which

Reverend Dewley plans a set of timetables detailing his every movement. Reverend Dewley dreams of a time when the government will adopt his ideas and everyone will live by timetable. This is, of course, exactly what has happened in the One State—Zamyatin's future society in *We*. Almost every hour is ruled by the Table of Hourly Commandments.

Islanders was in many ways a starting point for *We* and not least in Zamyatin's often extraordinary use of language. He firmly believed that literature could only be kept alive by constant innovation and revolution. His work is full of imagery and symbolism. Characters are reduced to a pair of worm-like lips or a glittering pince-nez. The lumbering Campbell is a lorry and the rigid Mr Craggs a little iron monument.

Such devices make the stories very funny, although under the humour lurks a nightmare of lifelessness. But though the Reverend Dewley may triumph, as long as there are dreams and laughter his world will always be under threat.

S. F. and J. S.

ISLANDERS

I

A FOREIGN BODY

The author of the *Precepts of Compulsory Salvation* was of course none other than the Reverend Dewley, the pride of Jesmond. Timetables drawn up in accordance with the *Precepts* were hung about the wall of Mr Dewley's study. A timetable for the consumption of food; a timetable for days of penance (two a week); a timetable for the use of fresh air; a timetable for charitable activities and finally, among the others, one timetable, out of a regard for decency left untitled, which particularly concerned Mrs Dewley and on which every third Saturday was marked.

At first there were occasions when Mrs Dewley went off the rails and would attempt on an unprescribed day to sit on the vicar's knees or act charitably at the wrong time. But each time Mr Dewley with characteristic tact and a dazzling golden smile (eight of his teeth were crowned) would explain, 'My dear, of course it's only a trifling transgression. But you must recall the second chapter of my *Precepts*; life must be like a well-run machine and lead us to our goal with mechanical inevitability, mechanical, you understand. And if even the smallest cog disturbs its working . . . Well, you understand, of course.'

Of course Mrs Dewley did understand. Once more she settled down by the window with a book. Her life went on, and between the chapters of her book she felt how dreary it was. A year later she was surprised to notice in the mirror that lines were appearing around her eyes. After only one year! Day after day she found herself unable to read. She sat by the window in a strange state of expectation, looking at the street, the people getting off the red tram and the full-blown clouds swiftly passing by. Mr Dewley, guided by his watch, was busy with his penance, physical labour and charitable acts, and rejoiced at how smoothly and exactly the machine was running.

Unfortunately, no machine is exempt from breaking down when a foreign body gets caught in its wheels. This happened once even to Reverend Dewley's machine.

It happened one Sunday in March whilst Mr Dewley was returning home from the morning service at the Church of St Enoch. Bicycles hummed past and Mr Dewley frowned at the importunate ringing of their bells, at the sun which was shining much too brightly and at the inexcusable chattering of the sparrows.

Mr Dewley was crossing the street to his house when suddenly a red motor car came round the corner. The vicar stopped and folding his arms behind him, as he often did, moved his fingers as though counting something; firstly, secondly, thirdly. When he reached thirdly he saw that somebody was walking slowly in front of the onrushing red motor car. There was only half a second, but the vicar could still see that he was walking slowly and had time to notice the huge square shoes stepping out slowly and relentlessly, like a lorry.

The red motor car shrieked again, the square shoes shot strangely through the air and the car stopped. Immediately the whole street was brought to a standstill. People crowded together, craning their heads: blood. A policeman calmly took the number of the motor car. A red-haired gentleman from among the onlookers loomed over the driver, shouting and waving his arms so that it seemed that he had at least four of them.

'Carry him into the house, then,' shouted the man with four arms. 'Whose house is it? Carry him in.'

It was only at this point that the vicar came to and said to himself, 'It's my house', grasped the square shoes and began to help carrying the injured man—*past* the door. But the ruse was unsuccessful.

'Hello, Reverend Dewley,' shouted the four-armed gentleman. 'You'll let us take him into your house, of course.'

The vicar smiled to reveal four of his gold teeth.

'Ah, O'Kelly, it's you. Of course, by all means, carry him in. These motor cars—it's simply dreadful. You don't know whose it is, do you?'

But O'Kelly was already somewhere inside, and the square dead soles of the man who liked to go for walks under motor cars swayed before the vicar, who followed on behind, anxiously twisting his fingers. 'Lunch. Two pages of commentary on the *Precepts*. Half an hour in the park. Visiting the sick . . .'

All this was no more. Reverend Dewley's great machine had ground to a halt. The light grey carpet in the spare bedroom was spattered with blood and a foreign body was installed in the bed which had been empty for years. Now the doctor would have to come. Lunch at a quarter past one was already long past and the vicar racked his brains over his timetable. If everything was moved forward three hours, then dinner would have to be at eleven in the evening and visiting the sick at one in the morning. The position was absurd and hopeless.

When the vicar was working in his study it was, of course, strictly forbidden to enter. So that if Mrs Dewley was now knocking at the door, it must be something important.

'Imagine, Edward, it's unheard of.' Mrs Dewley's cheeks were burning. 'The doctor's here but Campbell refuses to undress. You must say something to him. It's simply unheard of.'

'Who is Campbell? Him upstairs?' The vicar raised his eyebrows into a triangle.

Him upstairs, Campbell, was now lying with his eyes open. The doctor had washed his fair hair which had been caked with blood. It turned out that his head was unharmed but blood was coming from his throat. There was some kind of internal injury. But Campbell flatly refused to take off his jacket.

'Listen here, you can't carry on like this . . . For goodness sake. I mean, the doctor has to find out what's the matter.'

Mr Dewley looked with hatred at Campbell's heavy

square chin, which he was shaking stubbornly.

'Listen here, after all, you are in someone else's house. You're keeping us all waiting.' Mr Dewley smiled, baring the gold of his eight cruel teeth.

The chin twitched. Campbell grew even paler. 'Very well. In that case, I agree. But the lady must leave the room.'

The vicar and the doctor undid Mr Campbell's jacket. Under the jacket appeared a starched shirt-front and then an immoderately large bony body. There was no shirt. Improbable though it sounds, there was no shirt.

'Eh?' the vicar raised his eyebrows in displeasure and glanced questioningly at the doctor. But the doctor was busy. He was carefully feeling along the patient's right side.

Below in the drawing-room, the vicar rushed at the doctor.

'Well then, how is he?'

'Mmm . . . You must excuse me, nothing serious . . .' The doctor kept buttoning and unbuttoning his frock-coat. 'Two ribs, it may be worse. You must excuse me, but it will be clear what is wrong in about three days. Only he mustn't be moved.'

Mr Dewley made to cry out, 'What do you mean, not move . . .?' but quickly smiled a golden smile.

'Poor young man.'

All evening Mr Dewley wandered from room to room, adrift, feeling just like a train that has come off the rails and is lying with its wheels in the air above the embankment. Mrs Dewley was rushing about with ice and towels. Mrs Dewley was busy. The abandoned train was left to its own devices.

At half past eleven Reverend Dewley went off to bed, not so much to sleep as to express his views to Mrs Dewley before sleeping. But Mrs Dewley's bed was as yet empty. It was the first time this had happened in the ten years of their conjugal life and the vicar was astounded. He lay staring with eyes as unblinking as a fish's at the white emptiness of the bed next to him and in the emptiness some kind of shapes were forming. The clock struck midnight.

And then something very strange happened: the Mrs Dewley formed here—a negative Mrs Dewley—had an effect on the vicar which the bodily Mrs Dewley had never had. He wanted immediately, this very minute, to disrupt one of the timetables—immediately to see and feel Mrs Dewley.

The vicar sat up and called out, but no one answered: Mrs Dewley was busy there at the bedside of the sick, possibly dying man. How could one object to her fulfilling her duty to be compassionate?

The clock ticked on. The vicar lay with his arms carefully crossed on his chest as recommended in the *Precepts of Salvation* and tried to convince himself that he was asleep. When the clock struck two, the author of the *Precepts* heard himself saying something quite improper concerning 'these types with no shirts'. Fairness demands it be noted that immediately the author of the *Precepts* mentally raised his finger and noted the offensive occurrence by writing on a graph entitled 'Penance': Wednesday, 9 to 10 in the evening.

2

PINCE-NEZ

Mrs Dewley was short-sighted and wore pince-nez. They were the sort without frames, made from the very best glass which shone coldly as crystal. The pince-nez transformed Mrs Dewley into a magnificent example of a bespectacled woman, the mere sight of whom is enough to make one catch cold, just as one does from sitting in a draught. But it has to be said that it was this very draught which had in its time conquered the heart of Mr Dewley: he had his own way of looking at things. Be that as it may, it was certainly the case that Mrs Dewley's pince-nez were a vital and indispensable organ. In talking of Mrs Dewley, people who were little acquainted with her (visitors, naturally) would say, 'Ah Mrs

Dewley . . . she wears pince-nez.' For it was impossible to imagine Mrs Dewley without pince-nez. But now, however . . .

In the turmoil and anarchy of that day when a foreign body had invaded the vicar's home—on that fateful day, Mrs Dewley lost her pince-nez. Now she was unrecognisable: the pince-nez were like a shell which had broken and there was a new gleam in her straining eyes, her lips were half open, she was distracted and blissful.

The vicar positively didn't recognise Mrs Dewley.

'Listen, my dear, shouldn't you sit down and read for a while? You can't go on like this.'

'How can I without my pince-nez?'

Mrs Dewley brushed him aside and ran upstairs again to the injured man.

Probably because she was without her pince-nez, Campbell felt no kind of draught in her presence and when he began to improve he was glad to chat with her for hours. However, 'chatting' for Campbell meant no more than ten words a minute: he did not talk but crawled along, slowly lurching like a heavily laden truck with the broadest of wheels.

Mrs Dewley repeatedly tried to elicit some kind of information from him about the car accident.

'Well, yes, that's all very well. But you must have seen the car. Surely you could have moved out of the way. So why didn't you?'

'Er, yes, I saw it of course,'—the wheels squeaked—'but I was certain the car would stop.'

'But what if it couldn't stop, I mean simply couldn't?'

There was a pause. Slowly and heavily the truck rolled onwards without wavering an inch.

'It ought to have stopped.' Campbell wrinkled his forehead, puzzled: how could it not stop if he, Campbell, was sure it would stop? And faced with his, Campbell's, certainty, what signified the fact that his ribs were undeniably broken?

Mrs Dewley opened her eyes wider and looked closely at Campbell. Somewhere below, the abandoned train of the vicar sighed. Dusk poured in, flooding Campbell's bed and soon there was only a stubborn square shoe floating on its surface, protruding from under the blankets. (Campbell would not for anything take off his shoes.) Campbell talked and rolled on with a square conviction. Everything for him was indisputable and unshakeable: there was a God in heaven who obeyed the laws of nature; the greatest nation on earth was the British; the greatest crime on earth was to drink tea with the teaspoon still in the cup. And he, Campbell, the son of the late Sir Harold Campbell, could not possibly work as a common workman, or ask anyone for money—surely that was obvious.

'... We have been paying off my great-grandfather Sir Charles's debts. First my grandfather, then my father and then me. I had to sell the last of our properties, and now I've paid it all off.'

'And did you go hungry?'

'But I've already told you, it's quite clear, I couldn't possibly ...' Campbell fell into an offended silence.

But Mrs Dewley—she was without her pince-nez—bent lower and saw that Campbell's upper lip was pouting childishly. His stubborn chin and offended lip, they were so funny and at the same time so ... She wanted to take hold of him and hug him to her.

'There, there, darling, don't take on so, what a funny little thing you are ...'

But instead of this, Mrs Dewley asked, 'I hope you're feeling better today, Campbell? You can move your arms already, can't you? We'll see what the doctor says tomorrow ...'

In the morning the doctor arrived in his frock-coat, humble and timid as a rabbit.

'You see, constitution's the thing. Excuse me, but you have an excellent constitution,' muttered the doctor, looking down at his instrument bag and dropping it on the floor in his fright as the lawyer, O'Kelly, burst noisily into the room.

O'Kelly with his Irish red hair and multitude of waving arms made the room seem immediately loud and colourful.

'Well then Campbell, you're on the mend already? Of course, you English have heads made of some extraordinary stuff. It's the result of boxing. Have you ever boxed? A little? Well there you are then . . .'

Loud and colourful, it was only as he was leaving that O'Kelly realised that his waistcoat was undone and that in fact he had come on business: the owner of the motor car was ready to pay Campbell forty pounds on the spot. Campbell was not in the least surprised.

'Oh, I never doubted . . .'

He simply asked for pen and paper and wrote someone's address on one of Mrs Dewley's narrow ice-blue envelopes.

Two days later an answer arrived. And whilst Campbell was reading it, Mrs Dewley once more remembered her pince-nez. Suddenly, that very minute, she needed them and anxiously searched the room for the tenth time.

'I hope it's good news. I noticed it was a woman's handwriting . . .' Mrs Dewley rummaged furiously through the medicine cabinet.

'Oh yes, it's from my mother. I wrote to her about the money. Now she can settle down decently.'

Mrs Dewley slammed the cabinet shut.

'You can't imagine how pleased I am, so frightfully pleased for her.' Mrs Dewley really was pleased, one could see she was: her cheeks were flushed again.

At breakfast Mrs Dewley, gazing somewhere beyond the vicar, perhaps at the clouds, suddenly and unexpectedly smiled.

'You're in a good mood today, my dear . . .' The vicar revealed two of his gold crowns. 'Doubtless your patient is improving at last.'

'Oh yes, the doctor thinks that he will be able to get up on Sunday.'

'Well, that's splendid, simply splendid.' All eight of the vicar's gold crowns shone forth. 'At last we can begin to lead an ordered life again.'

'Yes. By the way,' Mrs Dewley frowned, 'when will my pince-nez be ready? Can't I have them by Sunday?'

3

SUNDAY GENTLEMEN

By Sunday the stone steps of the houses in Jesmond had as usual been scrubbed to a dazzling whiteness. The houses were old and smoke-blackened but the steps shone in white rows, like the Sunday gentlemen's false teeth. The Sunday gentlemen were of course manufactured at a factory in Jesmond, and on a Sunday morning thousands of copies appeared on the streets, along with the Sunday edition of the *St Enoch Parish Gazette*. Carrying identical canes and wearing identical top hats, the respectable Sunday gentlemen in their false teeth strolled down the street and greeted their doubles.

'Splendid weather, isn't it?'

'Oh yes, yesterday was far worse.'

Then the gentlemen listened to the Reverend Dewley's sermon about the tax collector and the Pharisee. Leaving the church, by some miracle they were able to find their own houses among the thousands of identical houses produced by the factory. They ate their dinner unhurriedly, talking to the family about the weather. Then they sang hymns with the family and waited until evening to go visiting with the family.

On Sunday morning Campbell astounded the doctor by getting up and leaving for his mother's. Mrs Dewley spent all day sitting at her usual window. It was impossible to read; her pince-nez had not been ready by Sunday.

'Never mind, they'll soon be ready and we can begin to lead an ordered life again,' she thought in the words of the vicar. She looked out of the window as the swift, full-blown clouds scudded past and she wanted to run after them so much that she could not tear her eyes away.

'The guests are already here, you know, my dear.' The vicar ran in, rubbing his hands. He was in excellent spirits: soon his ordered life would begin again. Mrs Dewley went off somewhere and talked about the weather to some pink and blue ladies while all the time the clouds were swelling and scudding past. The gold of the vicar's eight crowns were shining and he began to expound the ideas of the *Precepts of Compulsory Salvation* to the pink and blue ladies, which meant his barometer had reached maximum. Wasn't it in fact absolutely obvious? If the individual will, which was always unprincipled and disorderly, were to be exchanged for the will of the Great Machine of State, then with a mechanical inevitability, mechanical, you understand . . . And a head as round as a football nodded mechanically in reply.

The doorbell jangled. The clouds thickened and appeared in the semi-darkness of the hall: out of them emerged Campbell. He was cleanly shaven (which made his chin even squarer) and wearing a dinner-jacket, albeit a threadbare one. Behind him someone else appeared in the doorway. And when she stepped forward, Campbell proclaimed, 'My mother, Lady Campbell.'

They all turned around at once and fell silent, as if something embarrassing and unpleasant had happened, although there was nothing of the kind. For there was nothing remarkable about Lady Campbell's evening dress: it was simply a dress of grey silk, perhaps just a little old-fashioned. Still everyone was silent.

Lady Campbell slowly made her entrance. An invisible bridle was continually pulling her head upwards. She had yellowish-grey hair and her low-necked grey dress revealed the movement of ghastly, mummified shoulders and great bones. They stuck out like the skeleton of an old umbrella broken by the wind.

'So glad to have the honour . . .' the vicar began respectfully. 'This motor car accident has made it possible . . .' The vicar looked at her face: it was the most ordinary of faces, but there was a certain something . . .

'My late husband, Sir Harold, always objected to motor cars.' The invisible bridle pulled her head still higher. 'He found something positively ill-bred in their excessive speed.'

A very astute observation: that was it exactly—ill-bred. The vicar rubbed his hands. 'I quite agree with you, my dear Lady Campbell. That's it exactly: ill-bred.'

Yes, it was obvious. They were destined to become friends. The vicar scrutinised her face: no, there was nothing particular about it, it had only seemed so.

'I'm very pleased that Mrs Dewley gets on so well with my son. It's such a pleasure to watch them, isn't it?' Lady Campbell smiled.

At that moment the vicar realised it was her *lips*. They were pale pink, very thin and unusually long; they wriggled like worms, moving their tails up and down.

Mrs Dewley was talking animatedly about something and leaning close to Campbell's face—she was without her pince-nez.

'Her pince-nez are still not ready, you know . . .' the vicar muttered with embarrassment. The worms wriggled right at him. He took a step backwards and tried to think of something to say.

'Yes . . . Mr Campbell has probably told you: he received an offer to work for O'Kelly, the lawyer. Of course, it's not much, but for the time being . . .'

'Ah, necessity, of course, forces him to accept but all the same . . . O'Kelly! I've been here a year now, you know.' Lady Campbell smiled. The worms stretched and wriggled as they took aim at their victim. The vicar felt calm again. He was once more the author of the *Precepts of Salvation* and he benevolently revealed his gold crowns.

'The only hope lies with the beneficial influence of money. I shouldn't like to take all the credit for it myself, but the parishioners of St Enoch have reached exceptional heights and I hope that gradually even O'Kelly . . .'

'O'Kelly? Yes, isn't it awful?' fretted the pink and blue ladies. The head as round as a football nodded energetically. The football belonged to Mr MacIntosh and Mr MacIntosh, as is well known, knew everything.

'O'Kelly? What do you expect? Always backstage at the Empire . . . Secretaries? I mean to say, four secretaries?' Mr

MacIntosh bounced like a ball from corner to corner, in a dinner-jacket and a red, yellow and blue kilt, he bounced round the room with bare knees. Mr MacIntosh held the post of secretary of the Society of Honourable Bellringers of the Parish of St Enoch and consequently was an expert on moral issues.

'You know what I'd like to do with O'Kelly's sort . . .' MacIntosh grew animated. But unfortunately the sentence remained unpronounced: the accused appeared in person, and sentences of the court on moral issues are passed *in absentia*.

'We were just talking about you.' The vicar showed the lawyer two of his golden teeth.

'I am sure you were *duly* just to me,' laughed O'Kelly: he used the word *duly* and each time he used it, he annoyed the vicar.

'If you hadn't been late, my dear O'Kelly, you could have found out for yourself. But you're quite hopeless where punctuality is concerned.'

'I'm always punctual in my lateness: that's a sort of punctuality.' O'Kelly shook his red locks. As usual he was dishevelled, his jacket was covered in fluff, and one of his buttons was quite indecently undone. The pink and blue ladies nudged each other and Lady Campbell's worms twitched. It was only Mrs Dewley, perhaps, who saw none of this.

'So, you'll be moving into your rooms tomorrow morning. This is your last night with us.' Mrs Dewley's shoulders shivered: she had probably caught a cold.

Campbell stood in silence, with his legs stubbornly apart. Mrs Dewley glanced in the mirror opposite to set her hair right and it gleamed gold, the gold of the last leaves. She shuddered and laughed. 'Just suppose you were still ill and I was coming as usual to give you your compress for the night.'

'But I'm not ill any more.' Campbell frowned in perplexity; the lorry only drove along solid rock, the heavy wheels had got stuck in that unsteady word 'suppose'.

They sat down to dinner. MacIntosh spent a long time fussing about: it was a very delicate operation sitting down so as not to crumple his blue, yellow and green kilt. Once installed, Mr MacIntosh nodded his football head profoundly. 'Indeed, it's a great mystery, food, isn't it?'

This was very well put: a mystery. The great mystery flowed on in silence, and only where O'Kelly sat was it red, gaudy and noisy. He was talking about Paris, about some inflatable suitcase he had bought there especially to get round the English law. '. . . You see over here, without luggage they won't let you into a hotel with a woman. And so you whip it out of your pocket, blow it up and—pfff—there you have a perfect suitcase. After all, ladies, isn't the role of the law the same as that of your dresses? Oh excuse me, Reverend.'

The vicar raised his eyebrows into a triangle and once more looked at his watch: on the Sunday timetable for sleeping the figure eleven was marked. And apart from this O'Kelly . . .

The mystery was drawing to a close. The Sunday gentlemen hurried home with their wives.

Saying goodbye to Campbell by the door of his bedroom, Mrs Dewley laughed again and the candle in her hand shook. 'Shall I bring you a compress then?'

'No, I'm quite well. Why should I need a compress?' The candle lit up Campbell's immutable, square chin.

Mrs Dewley quickled turned and went off to her bedroom. The vicar was already asleep in a white flannel nightcap, his arms crossed on his chest.

In the morning at breakfast the vicar saw Mrs Dewley wearing her pince-nez and was positively delighted. 'Well now, at last I recognise you!'

4

A HIGHER BREED OF INTELLECT

Mr O'Kelly's office was situated on the second floor of an old house. In the thick stone wall there was an iron-plated door with a knocker. A dark stone staircase led up to the office and a step down out into Cobbler John's Alley. The alley was a narrow crack between the houses where only two people could pass, and above was a strip of blue sky between the walls. The irrepressible Cobbler John had once lived in the old house, stubbornly adhering to the Lutheran heresies for which he was burned. Now Mr Campbell had come to work here.

In the first small room four young ladies were bashing away on Underwoods. O'Kelly led Campbell to the first of them and introduced him. 'My wife Cecily, she's a lamb.'

With her flaxen hair and tiny little mouth, she was indeed like an Easter lamb with a ribbon round its neck. Campbell carefully shook her hand. Then O'Kelly introduced him to the other three and with the same terse seriousness said of each one, 'My wife. My wife. My wife.'

Campbell stopped with his hand outstretched, and frowned as though in pain. The lorry panted audibly, unable to move on. My wife. My wife. My wife . . . He looked at O'Kelly, but O'Kelly was completely serious.

O'Kelly came to his aid. 'Listen here, surely you know, I'm a Mohammedan.'

With relief, Campbell ceased frowning: now both a major and a minor premise were to hand—a complete syllogism. Everything became simple as a square.

'Oh well, I respect every kind of established religion,' Campbell began seriously, 'every kind.'

For a minute O'Kelly reddened as he silently filled with laughter. Then he exploded, as did his four wives.

'Listen, Campbell . . . Oh, it's too much. You're such a . . . Oh Lord, I don't believe it . . . My God, he swallowed it whole. Well, my lad, I'll soon teach you to know a lie when you hear one.'

A lie? Campbell was hopelessly lost. A lie? He couldn't understand. Whether it was a joke or the truth, it was simply beyond comprehension, in the way the unimaginable infinity of the universe is beyond comprehension. Campbell stood crushed, with his legs apart like two pillars.

'Listen here, Campbell, let's be serious.' O'Kelly became serious, as he always did when he was not talking seriously. 'Don't forget that we lawyers, we're a higher breed of intellect, and so it's our privilege to lie. It's as clear as day. Animals can't even imagine lying: if you were to find yourself among some wild islanders, they too would only speak the truth until they learned about European culture. Ergo, this is a sign that . . .'

All this was absolutely the case. But Campbell was unshakeably, squarely convinced that it ought not to be true, and as a result his head felt as though it would burst. He had already stopped listening to O'Kelly's words, and simply helplessly pawed at his forehead with his hand in the way a bear paws at the bees that are clinging to him.

A young lady was waiting for the lawyer in the waiting-room. Her hair was cut like a boy's and she was smoking a cigarette.

'Ah, Didi! Have you been waiting long, little one? Mrs Didi Lloyd, a client of ours. A divorce case . . .' The lawyer turned to Campbell, saw his brow trying to grasp it all and rushed on, 'I said to her, "start by making a trial marriage," but she wouldn't listen . . . Haven't you heard of trial marriages? Well, of course, a Bill was passed in Parliament on the 31st . . . Yes, on the 31st of March.'

Mrs Didi Lloyd was easily amused; her lips were trembling. Again Campbell was lost as to whether to believe him or not, but O'Kelly was already spreading out some documents before him.

'There are only odds and ends left; just sort them out.'

Campbell bowed very formally. Mrs Didi Lloyd's boyish behaviour, her cigarette and her crossed legs were not to his taste. He sat down to the documents and O'Kelly paced up and down behind him, sprinkling ash on to his waistcoat and listening attentively.

A document was something definite. The fog in Campbell's head cleared: the lorry pulled its load surely and swiftly along the well-travelled road. O'Kelly beamed and clapped Campbell on the back.

'Well done, I knew you could do it. You work like a horse . . .'

Clients came and went. O'Kelly was already beginning to yawn: it was time for dinner.

'Well now, how about a restaurant? And then we can go to the theatre. Why not? That's settled, then.'

Lady Campbell was expecting him home for dinner. But as usual O'Kelly had various crooked and unexpected arguments. In the end there was no way out of it and Campbell followed obediently.

At the theatre after a bottle of French wine Campbell felt very tall, taller than everyone, and light. He very rarely felt this light. He found it very pleasant and funny and swayed along to every thing on the stage, feeling like a five-year-old. Moreover, everyone was happily watching and laughing as if they too were five-year-olds. It was very amusing: a gentleman with a false nose was dancing the two-step with a fat woman. Then they started quarrelling over a shilling they had found. And the gentleman with the nose slapped the woman across the face while a drum in the orchestra beat in time. Then a girl, spotlit in turn by a red and then a green light, played some Mozart on a violin. Then a slim woman dressed in black slowly did a sort of floating dance in the semi-darkness.

Once, when she turned, Campbell was amazed to see that he recognised the delicate boyish face with short curls: no, it couldn't be! But she was already behind a brightly lit screen and her shadow gradually cast off everything with a habitual slowness: stockings, suspenders and top. Now came her next dance—in red.

'Mrs Didi Lloyd?' asked Campbell, not taking his eyes off the screen.

'Mrs . . .' O'Kelly jeered. 'Yes, of course it's Didi.'

O'Kelly looked curiously out of the corner of his eye at Campbell who was straining forward. Now the lorry was gathering speed and about to run over everything in its path.

Didi finished the red dance. Campbell at last drew breath and did it so noisily, from deep inside, that he frightened himself and looked round. From the box on his right something shone out at him from the darkness.

'So then, old man, looks as though you enjoyed it,' smirked O'Kelly.

Dressed once more, in a coat and hat, Didi made her way down the aisle towards them. She sat down next to O'Kelly and laughing breathlessly, whispered something in his ear. It felt strange to see her dressed now, and, besides, he thought she was laughing too loudly. Campbell drew away, stuck out his chin and sat upright and unshakeable, stubbornly listening to a piece played on a strange instrument made of one string stretched along a mop handle.

The lights went up. Didi turned to Campbell. 'Listen, Campbell, is it true what O'Kelly says, that you've never . . . you've never . . .' She took Campbell by the hand and with a tiny gold pencil began to write something on his cuff.

'What if my mother . . .?' Campbell recalled the very thin, wriggling lips and again he looked round, as though Lady Campbell might be there. But instead of Lady Campbell, in the box on the right he saw Mrs Dewley. It seemed that the glass in her pince-nez shone with a cold light directly upon Campbell. But evidently it only seemed so: shining directly at him, Mrs Dewley did not bow. Obviously she had not seen him.

5

ABOUT THE CHINA PUG

The china pug lived at number 72, in Mrs Aunty's furnished rooms. Here the lodgers changed every week—every time a new revue came to the Empire. There were always clouds of tobacco smoke. At night someone would be splashing and laughing in the bath. The blinds in the bedrooms were lowered until midday. But Johnny the china pug was not in the least put out by this and frcm the height of the mantelpiece he gazed on life with his usual calm and knowing smile. Johnny the pug belonged to Didi, and, *vice versa*, Didi belonged to Johnny the pug. They were inseparable friends. So it was all the more disappointing that for no obvious reason Campbell immediately felt indifferent towards Johnny.

'Tell me, Campbell, why don't you love my Johnny? Look how charmingly ugly he is. And he's so faithful. You can do what you like with him . . .'

Campbell had some documents spread out on his knees. It was a very hard task to convince Didi to take the money that had so kindly been offered her by her former husband, Mr Lloyd. Campbell furrowed his brow painfully.

'Mr O'Kelly thinks that you ought to take the money. And I can't understand why . . .'

'Tell me, Campbell, don't you find that Johnny looks like Mr O'Kelly? They're both so sweetly ugly in exactly the same way, and so clever. And they smile in exactly the same way too. Look, sit here, from the side, do you see?'

Upright and unbending, Campbell sat down on the carpet, like a Buddha, and looked angrily at Johnny. But it was true—the pug was O'Kelly. They were as like as two peas. Slowly lurching, Campbell laughed loudly, dragging some kind of load behind him as he did so and swayed further and further. Didi was already talking about something else but it was impossible to calm him down.

There was something Byronic about Johnny. In fact, he was a deeply disenchanted creature and that was why he smiled his eternal smile. A book stood before Johnny, bound in white morocco, one of the few valuables that Didi had never pawned and Johnny was reading slowly and sadly. The firelight flickered on the furniture. The lamps were not yet lit; the forgotten papers shone white on the floor;

Campbell's square chin was bathed in red. Johnny read on . . .

Campbell recollected himself and angrily leapt up from the carpet. 'All the same, I have to tell Mr O'Kelly why you won't take the money.'

The little white book flew into a corner and the black line of her eyebrows sudenly brought out the boyishness of Didi's face. She shouted, 'Because it was I . . . I who was unfaithful to Mr Lloyd. Do you understand? And why was I unfaithful to him? Because the weather was fine. Please get out of here and take your papers with you! Johnny is ten times cleverer than you: he never asks any questions . . .'

In the morning at the office, Campbell complained with his lip pouting childishly, 'She simply won't listen . . . She's only interested in her pug.'

O'Kelly grinned like the pug. 'Oh Campbell, what a case you are . . . Get her round to my place tonight and we'll soon sort her out.'

It was a tranquil evening. The trees stood sedately and discreetly in the front gardens, cropped very closely, delighting the eye—rows of wooden soldiers. It must have been a holiday or simply a special service for the children: the bells of St Enoch's church pealed, one after the other and always in the same order—a handle was continually turning—and the closely-cropped children in their white collars walked along in sedate rows.

Campbell and Didi stopped to let the procession pass. The last white-collared row went past, and round the corner appeared the Reverend Dewley accompanied by Mrs Dewley and the secretary of the Honourable Bellringers, MacIntosh. The vicar strode along like a general: he was leading the white-collared army to salvation along the mathematically correct path. Behind his back he was slowly moving his fingers as though counting something. Campbell felt slightly uncomfortable: he hadn't been to the Dewleys since that Sunday. He ought to go up and say something.

'Excuse me, I won't be a minute.' Campbell left Didi by the church railings and slowly swayed over to meet the

Dewleys. Stubbornly placing his legs apart and looking awkwardly at his square shoes, Campbell apologised: he'd been terribly busy at the lawyer's. There simply hadn't been time to . . . Mrs Dewley's pince-nez shone like crystal; the vicar flashed his golden teeth and looked askance at Didi, who was standing by the railings and playing with Campbell's cane.

'Splendid evening,' Campbell observed cheerily. He screwed up his face as though in pain. There was a pause.

MacIntosh came to the rescue. He was universally acknowledged to be an original and profound man. At this moment he was looking studiously down at his feet.

'I often think what a great thing civilisation is. Take this pavement for example. Just think: a pavement.'

At this instant there was a peal of laughter and everyone turned round in horror. That young woman with the cane was laughing. She was always laughing at something. Now she was leaning on the cane and shaking, shaking with laughter, and her short curls shook too.

In fact, nothing further happened in particular: Mrs Dewley simply turned and looked at the young woman, or, to be more exact, not at her but at the church railings against which she was leaning. Mrs Dewley stared as though the woman were completely transparent, made of glass.

Didi spluttered. She wanted to say something—which would of course have been just too much—but simply shrugged her shoulders and quickly walked off. And then Mrs Dewley politely offered Campbell her hand. It seemed that her hand was shaking or perhaps it was Campbell's hand that was shaking.

'Goodbye, Mr Campbell. All the same, we hope to see you soon.' Mrs Dewley went on into the church.

It was unheard of . . . Campbell's ears were burning. He ran after Didi as fast as his weight could carry him. But it was as though the earth had swallowed her up. She was nowhere to be seen.

In the evening, after the service had ended, Mrs Dewley was sitting with the vicar in the dining-room and tapping the spine of her book.

'So much for your compulsory salvation. You can see which way Campbell's going. If I were you, I'd . . .'

The vicar lifted his eyebrows into a triangle. He positively didn't recognise Mrs Dewley. Previously she had shown no interest whatsoever in the *Precepts of Salvation*. The vicar rubbed his hands: this was a good sign. This was splendid: 'You're right, my dear. We must do something about it. Of course we must.'

Meanwhile, in number 72, the fireplace was covered in ash and the last warmth stirred and flickered beneath it. Didi lay on the carpet with Johnny the china pug. The pug's ugly muzzle was wet. Campbell stood in the doorway. His face was screwed up as if in pain. He had come to tell Didi that her behaviour was peculiar to say the least. And now he couldn't find the words, or something was in the way. They were caught in his throat. Really, it was absurd.

Campbell tried to construct a syllogism.

6

THE FACE OF A WELL-BRED MAN

It is common knowledge that a well-bred man should as far as possible have no face. That is to say, not so much be completely without one, but rather, should have a face and yet at the same time appear faceless. It should not stand out, just as a shirt made by a good tailor does not stand out. Needless to say, the face of a well-bred man should be exactly like that of other (well-bred) men and of course in no circumstances whatsoever should it alter. Naturally houses, trees, streets, sky and everything else in the world must satisfy the same conditions to have the honour of being known as respectable and well-bred. And so when the cool grey days had passed and suddenly it was summer and the sun shone scandalously bright, Lady Campbell felt shocked: 'There's something positively . . . goodness knows what's happening!' Lady Campbell's worms stirred and protruded, but the unbridled and ill-bred sun continued to grin broadly. And then Lady Campbell did the only thing she could. She let down all the venetian blinds and a more moderate and respectable light settled in the room. Lady Campbell and her son now occupied three rooms: two bedrooms upstairs and a dining-room downstairs overlooking the street. Everything had worked out splendidly. Lady Campbell understood the car accident to be a clear example of God's mercy. But then it was only to be expected: God does not abandon respectable people.

And now everything was just as it should be: the carpet, the fireplace and above the fireplace a portrait of Sir Harold with the same square Campbell chin, the mahogany table by the window and on the table a vase full of Sunday carnations. In the windows of all the houses on the left-hand side of the road there were green vases and on the right-hand side blue. Lady Campbell lived on the right-hand side and consequently she had a blue vase on her table.

As far as possible, Lady Campbell tried to reinstate the routine that had existed when the late Sir Harold was alive. In the morning, she laced herself into her corset, and at dinner appeared in evening dress. For five shillings she bought a small brass gong. And as the old housekeeper did not know how to beat the gong, Lady Campbell always beat it herself. She would lift the gong down from the dining-room wall, go out into the corridor, beat it and return to the dining-room. Even when eating alone, because Campbell was at the office, she still beat it: the main thing was order.

Unfortunately there was no footman to serve lunch and dinner, only old Mrs Taylor, ancient and trembling. And so that this should be even vaguely respectable, Lady Campbell tried to convince the old woman that she should serve dinner in white gloves.

'Lord above, more of her whims! You scrub your hands morning, noon and night and it's not good enough for them.' The old woman took offence and even burst into tears, but finally acquiesced for two shillings extra a month.

Now everything was in order and Lady Campbell asked

O'Kelly to dinner: let him see that he was not dealing with just anyone! There was a good deal of fuss and bother. Bottles and flowers graced the table. Old Mrs Taylor had washed her white gloves. Only O'Kelly . . .

It may be hard to believe, but O'Kelly appeared for dinner in a lounge suit. The entire dinner was spoiled. Lady Campbell's worms stretched and stirred.

'I'm so glad, Mr O'Kelly, that you've come dressed informally. Besides, with your cast of face, a dinner jacket really wouldn't . . .'

O'Kelly burst out laughing. 'Oh, I have a high opinion of my appearance. It's uniquely ugly, but it is unique, and that's all that matters.'

Fat and shortish, he was breathless from the heat and wiped his face with a gaudy handkerchief. His red curls were dishevelled, and his four arms spun unceasingly; he spilled sauce on his waistcoat and chattered incessantly. Yes, in fact, Wilde was also ugly, but drew attention to his ugliness and everyone thought it was beauty. And moreover, accentuated plainness and accentuated vice ought to bring about harmony. Beauty lies in harmony, in style, whether it be the harmony of ugliness or beauty, vice or virtue. But then O'Kelly noticed that the invisible bridle was tugging at Lady Campbell's yellow head. The pale pink worms stirred and crept ominously. O'Kelly stopped short and the pale pink worms also stopped. To think of mentioning Wilde in company! And if Lady Campbell spared O'Kelly this time, it was only for the sake of her son.

Old Mrs Taylor brought in the liqueurs and coffee with her trembling hands in their white gloves. Lady Campbell had given much thought to the liqueurs. But in the end she decided to put off the repair of her shoes for a month. One could not manage without liqueurs or without a gong, or Mrs Taylor's white gloves. Twice Lady Campbell pushed the liqueurs towards O'Kelly and twice he poured himself a Scotch whisky.

The liqueurs, O'Kelly's bright hair, and his arms spinning in the air—all this combined to irritate Lady Campbell.

The worms bit each other: 'I must say, you are original: it's the first time I've seen a man who drinks whisky with his coffee.'

To Lady Campbell, 'original' had the same ring as 'ill-bred'. But Mr O'Kelly was obviously too thick-skinned. He was cheerfully silent for a moment—for he was even silent cheerfully—and then he thought aloud: 'In this sort of heat, it would be good to prance about in just a kilt.' That reminded him of something, and he told them how he and a Scottish friend had walked around Paris. The little Parisian boys had in the end been unable to resist: they waited for an opportune moment, and then lifted the kilt to see if there was anything underneath in the way of underpants, or whether . . .

Lady Campbell could simply stand no more. She stood up incensed, walked to the door, and called to her foam-white cat, Milly, 'Milly, come away from here . . . Milly, there's nothing for you here. So what are you doing in here? Your milk is in the corridor.'

But the spoilt Milly was clearly not averse to listening to O'Kelly's stories. She was mewing and rubbing against him. Lady Campbell stooped down: out sprang her collar-bones, her shoulder-blades and various other bones—the entire skeleton of the broken umbrella. Lady Campbell proceeded out of the door with Milly under her arm.

Majestic and terrible, mummy-like in her décolleté, she appeared again only when O'Kelly was lumbering around the hall looking for his stick (which he had not brought). Campbell left with O'Kelly.

The pale sky was folded in and concave as often happens at twilight after a hot day. Campbell shuddered, partly from the cold, and partly at the inevitable discussions about what was and was not respectable which would follow tomorrow with Lady Campbell. He shuddered, but still he walked on with O'Kelly to number 72. In the main, he was entirely in agreement with Lady Campbell: it was not at all respectable at Mrs Aunty's furnished rooms. Things were not what he was used to. They stuck out and got in the way, as would a stone in the middle of one of Jesmond's asphalted streets. But still he walked on.

'Seeing as O'Kelly's going. I must keep on good terms with him,' Campbell reassured himself.

As usual, at number 72 the fire was lit. Didi was sitting in front of the fire on the carpet, drying her curly boyish hair. The pages of a letter were scattered on the floor and Johnny the pug was smiling down on them. O'Kelly almost stepped on the pages. He bent down and picked them up.

'Don't touch!' Didi shouted angrily. 'I tell you, don't touch them! Don't you dare touch them!'

Her brows met. The boyish face disappeared and became the face of a woman burning with a dark fire.

O'Kelly sat down on a low pouffe and began to jabber. 'It's no good, it's no good, my girl. Lady Campbell has just informed us that the face of a well-bred person should be as immutable as . . . as eternity or as the British constitution. And by the way, have you heard that Parliament is introducing a Bill to make all Englishmen have noses of the same length? Yes, it's the only irregularity left, which must of course be eliminated. And then they will be identical, like buttons, like Ford motor cars, like ten thousand copies of *The Times*. A grand scheme, to say the least . . .'

Didi did not smile. She still held on to the sheets and her eyebrows were drawn together just as firmly as her fingers clutched the sheets. And Campbell did not smile: something was seething within him, seething, beating. It grew beyond control and he stood up. He took two steps towards Didi and asked in a tone which he should not have used, 'What is this letter? Why mustn't he lay a finger on it? It's . . .' He spoke and heard himself with astonishment: it wasn't him, but then who was it? And for a second Didi listened with astonishment. Then her brows drew apart. She fell on to the carpet and choked with laughter:

'Oh Campbell, I think you're . . . Johnny, my little pug, you know, Campbell . . . he's . . .'

7
THE STEERING BREAKS DOWN

At last the matter of the divorce ended, and now nobody had any rights over Didi excepting, of course, Johnny the china pug. The three of them celebrated the event together: O'Kelly, Didi and Campbell. They dined in a private room, and drank. O'Kelly clambered on to the chair and proposed toasts, waving his multitude of arms. Everything was bright and colourful and made the head spin. Somehow no one felt like going home. They decided to go on to the fight.

The taxi raced along as though possessed, or at least it seemed to. Every time it turned a corner it lurched, and several times Campbell scorched himself against Didi's knee. The taxi flew on.

'You know,' Campbell remembered, 'several times I've dreamed that I'm in a motor car and the steering isn't working. I drive through fences, through whatever comes in my way, and the main thing is that . . .'

But he did not manage to tell them what the main thing was. They were already entering the hall. A steep fan of benches was full to overflowing. Once more Campbell felt cramped and hot. He'd been scorched and it was as if the taxi was still flying on. 'I shouldn't drink so much.'

'Listen, Campbell, what are you thinking about?' shouted O'Kelly. 'Did you hear? Sergeant Smith, the champion of England. Imagine: Smith! Look! There!'

They stepped forward slowly from the two opposite corners of the four-cornered ring. Smith was tall with a small, fair head: a sort of small unnecessary ornament on his huge shoulders. And Bourne from Jesmond, with a protruding jaw and the look of a hardened killer.

'Hurrah! Come on, Bourne! Jesmond! Sergeant Smith! Hurrah!'

The whole twenty rows of benches stamped and whistled and seethed. The snake's twenty coils shook and overflowed. Then suddenly it froze and stretched its head forward: the referee in the ring took off his top hat. Looking out from under the grey peak of his eyebrows, he announced the rules: 'Ladies and gentlemen, there will be twenty three-minute rounds, and half a minute's rest after each round, in accordance with the Queensbury Rules.'

The referee rang the bell. Smith and Bourne slowly approached each other. Bourne was wearing black trunks and Smith blue. They smiled and shook hands: to show that whatever happened was only the sport of well-bred people who respected each other. And then suddenly, black Bourne stuck out his jaw and began to circle Smith.

'That's it, Jesmond. Good shot!' they shouted from above, when Bourne punched a red mark on the English champion's chest. The twenty-coiled snake wound tighter and its breathing quickened. Campbell saw Didi stir and crane forward. He too craned forward, caught in the snake's coils.

The referee, with his peaked brows, sounded the bell. Black and blue, both stretched out on the stools, each in his corner. Their mouths gaped open like stranded fish, and they hurried to gulp down as much air as possible in half a minute. The seconds fussed about, sprinkled their tongues with water, and waved their towels. The half minute passed. They fell to once more. Smith seized a moment to catch Bourne's nose from below with his heavy fist. Bourne hid his face in Smith's armpit and circled the ring with him so as to protect his face from being hit. Blood flowed from Bourne's nose, staining Smith's trunks. The two bare bodies circled and floundered. The snake stretched forward, growing more and more convulsive, to drink in the smell of blood. All around there was stamping and indistinct roaring.

'Give him a kiss under the arm, Bourne. That's a tasty spot,' shouted a piercing, boyish voice.

Didi, agitated and red in the face, clutched Campbell's sleeve. Campbell tore himself away from the ring and looked at her. His nostrils flared eagerly and his square chin jutted out fiercely. He was a different man, and somehow Didi felt small. What had she wanted to ask . . .? She had forgotten.

'Look, look!' O'Kelly shouted.

It was coming to an end. Bourne swayed from the blows and very slowly his legs softened, melted like wax, and he fell to the ground with a resounding crash. Jesmond was defeated. Jesmond howled: 'It's all wrong. He hit Bourne when he was down.'

'Down with Smith! It's not fair. We saw it all.'

Smith stood with his little head thrown back and smiled. He was waiting for them to be quiet.

'. . . And he's even got the nerve to grin. The cheek of it!'

Didi was fuming and trembling. She turned to Campbell and stung his elbow with something which nipped gently: 'If I was like you, I'd go up there and beat hell out of him.'

For a moment, Campbell looked her in the eye, and the bedevilled motor car broke free and tore away.

'Very well. I'll go.' He moved towards the platform.

This was unthinkable. It *shouldn't* be happening. Campbell didn't believe it but he couldn't stop himself. The steering was broken. The car hooted and tore through everything in its path. But was it a frightening or a pleasant sensation?

'Listen, you're not really going to . . . Campbell, are you off your head? Stop him, stop him, O'Kelly!'

But O'Kelly simply smiled silently like Johnny the china pug. The referee announced that Mr Smith had kindly agreed to five rounds with Mr Campbell of Jesmond. Campbell's great white body appeared in the ring and Jesmond roared ecstatically.

Mr Campbell of Jesmond was taller and heavier than Smith, but still, from the very first round it was clear that this escapade of his was sheer madness. Still smiling, Smith landed blows in his side and chest, which echoed hollowly somewhere up in the dome. But Campbell stood very firm, with his pillar-like legs stubbornly placed apart and his chin obstinately thrust forward.

'Listen, O'Kelly, he'll kill him. It's simply awful,' said Didi, not taking her eyes off him and growing pale. But O'Kelly just smiled silently his knowing smile.

By the third round, covered in red marks and blood,

Campbell was still holding out. In the silence an ecstatic voice shouted from above: 'His mug must be made of cast iron.'

All around the hall people snorted. Didi looked round indignantly, but silence had already fallen again—the fourth round had begun. At the very beginning of this round, Campbell fell.

Didi leaped up, her eyes wide open. The referee looked down from beneath the grey peak of his brows and counted the seconds:

'One, two, three, four . . .'

At the last second, the ninth, Campbell stood up obstinately. He took another blow, and everything began swimming in front of him. The last thing he saw was Didi's pale face.

Campbell could not remember clearly. They took him off somewhere. Didi was crying, O'Kelly laughing. Then they gave him something to drink. He fell asleep and woke up in the middle of the night. The moon was shining in the window and Johnny the ugly pug was grinning in Campbell's face.

It was Didi's room. Didi's room in the middle of the night . . . Was he delirious? Then slowly, through a fog, he thought, 'It's true, they couldn't have taken me home in such a . . .' His tongue was dry. He desperately wanted something to drink.

'Didi!' Campbell called out shyly.

A figure in black pyjamas got up from the sofa. 'Oh, at last, you've come to! Campbell, dearest, I'm so glad. I was so frightened . . . Can you forgive me?'

Didi sat on the bed and took Campbell's hands in her own hot little hands. There was a scent of stocks. Campbell closed his eyes. Campbell was no longer there. There was only his hand holding on to Didi. In the few square inches of this hand was contained everything that was Campbell, and it was drinking, drinking it all in.

'Didi, I only went . . . because . . . because . . .' His throat tightened, and he felt so heavy he could not move.

Didi leaned over. She was serious, both a girl and a mother. 'You are funny! I understand. You don't have to say.'

She stung Campbell with two gentle nips—quickly pecked him on the lip—and everything melted away and there was only the smell of stocks, pungent and sweet, as always in dry weather.

All night the smirking china pug watched over Campbell and hindered him from thinking. Campbell wrinkled his forehead painfully and racked his brains. The things familiar to him were laid out there in square boxes, and in one of them, a sacred one, lay: God, the British Nation, the address of his tailor and his future wife—Mrs Campbell, who looked like the portrait of Campbell's mother as a young woman. All these were actual objects, immutable and concrete. What had just happened would not fit into any box and so consequently . . .

But the steering was clearly not working. Campbell was driven on and on straight through this 'consequently' and through everything in his path.

In the morning Campbell woke up. Didi had already left, but the room smelled of her, and her black pyjamas lay across a chair. Campbell got up with difficulty, and struggled into yesterday's dinner-jacket. For a long while he gazed at the pyjamas, restrained himself, then fell on his knees, looked at the door and buried his face in the black silk, in the scent of stocks.

Didi arrived, fresh and full of life, with wet, tousled curls.

'Didi, I've been thinking about it all night,' Campbell placed his legs firmly apart. 'Didi, you must be my wife.'

'Do you think so? Must I?' Didi shook with laughter. 'Well then, if I must . . . Only for goodness sake, lie down. The doctor said to keep you in bed . . . for goodness sake . . . that's it . . .'

8

PINK AND BLUE

The fight was on Saturday, and by Monday Campbell's name was already enhancing the pages of the *Jesmond Star*.

> **SENSATION AT BOXING HALL!**
>
> **BOXER-ARISTOCRAT**
>
> The ring where only last week we saw the negro, Jones, has for the first time been graced by the presence of a boxer from an aristocratic family, albeit an impoverished one.
>
> Mr Campbell (son of the late H. D. Campbell) withstood the iron blows of Smith with astounding endurance, until finally in the fourth round, he fell a victim to his rash display of courage. Campbell was carried off unconscious. Among Mr Campbell's friends, D***, star of the Empire, stood out in her finery.

On that day in Jesmond, life was in full swing. The weather was hardly mentioned. Everyone's mind was taken up with Campbell. They talked only of the Campbell scandal. People stopped outside old Mrs Taylor's house and looked in at the Campbells' windows, as if they were expecting a sign. But no sign was forthcoming. Then they visited Lady Campbell and joyfully expressed their condolences.

'Oh, how awful, simply awful! Surely he wasn't so badly hurt that he couldn't be brought home to you?'

Lady Campbell's worms wriggled.

'Poor Lady Campbell! You can't even visit him. You can't possibly enter *that* house, can you?'

'And what's more—*that* woman! Dear Lady Campbell, we do understand.'

Lady Campbell's worms writhed and sizzled on a slow fire. The pink and blue ladies made much of it all. Then for some reason they hovered about the Reverend Dewley's house: their sharp sense of smell had picked up something there. Then they went to *that* house and particularly watched the curtain across the window. But the curtain was not drawn back.

However, the pink and blue ladies were mistaken about the Reverend Dewley's house: what happened there amounted to nothing. At breakfast, Mrs Dewley was reading the newspaper and accidentally upset her coffee cup. This can happen to anyone. The point was that the tablecloth had only been put out on Saturday, and the timetable did not permit a new one until next Saturday. It was no wonder the vicar was in a bad mood and went off to write a commentary on the *Precepts of Salvation*, while Mrs Dewley sat at the window and watched the red trams. Then she set off for *that* house, asked the landlady something, and immediately turned back (perhaps having received the answer that *that* woman was with Mr Campbell or that Mr Campbell was much better). But this of course is only conjecture and all that can be known for certain is that exactly at a quarter to one Mrs Dewley was at home, and at exactly a quarter to one lunch began. Clearly everything had gone well.

Everything happened in accordance with the timetable and at the vicar's house that evening there was the usual Monday meeting of the Society of Honourable Bellringers of the Parish of St Enoch and the editors of the parish gazette. There were several pink and blue ladies and the unfailing MacIntosh, in his blue, yellow and green kilt. Lady Campbell did not come.

Everyone was on tenterhooks. Campbell's name was on everybody's lips. But there was no arguing with the vicar: in front of him lay a list of questions requiring discussion—seventeen items—and of course not one could be left out.

'Ladies and gentlemen, your attention please: now a most serious matter.'

The matter concerned raising the profitability of the St Enoch parish gazette. The vicar had just acquired for the gazette the serial: 'Arsène Lupin's Adventures in Paris'. Subsequently this would of course increase sales, but meanwhile it was necessary to cover expenditure. What they needed were advertisements, advertisements and yet more advertisements.

'Mr MacIntosh, we await your help.'

Mr MacIntosh dealt in ladies' underwear. He had excellent connections. Immediately he gave them three addresses and tried hard to think of some more.

'Ah yes,' he remembered, 'what about Scribb's rubber products?'

The vicar raised his eyebrows: there was one serious condition.

'Mr MacIntosh, do remember that we guarantee the quality of what we recommend. The St Enoch parish gazette cannot . . .'

'Oh I can vouch for Scribb's products,' the secretary of the Society of Honourable Bellringers objected vehemently. 'I have personally . . .'

But the vicar stopped him with the slightest wave of his hand, the same he used in his sermons to depict the ascent of a righteous soul into heaven. Scribb's products were accepted; the vicar took down the appropriate address.

Lady Campbell arrived late, when everyone had ceased to expect her. As always, her head was pulled upwards by the invisible bridle. Her face was still more like a mummy; her bones pushed out still more sharply—the skeleton of an umbrella broken by the wind.

Like heavenly doves flying down after corn, the pink and blue ladies hovered around Lady Campbell: well, what had happened? What had she heard? The lips lay drawn and unmoving and at last they trembled with difficulty:

'All I can think is what my late husband, Sir Harold, would have said.'

She raised her eyes towards the place where God and Sir Harold dwelled. The two tiny tears which her code of conduct permitted her fell from her eyes and were quickly caught by her lawn handkerchief.

The two tears were met with profound silence. Mrs Dewley was standing apart, crumpling and smoothing out a bluish envelope. They remained silent: what could be said at such a moment and how could one help?

Then suddenly MacIntosh's football-like head emerged. As usual he was indispensable.

'Ladies and gentlemen, it's a difficult business, but we must ask the vicar to sacrifice himself. Anyone who heard the vicar's inspired sermon on Sunday will understand that only hearts of stone could . . . Ladies and gentlemen, we must ask the vicar to go to *that* house. And I am sure, we are sure . . .'

'Yes, we are sure,' chorused the pink and blue ladies.

Before replying, the vicar paused to blow his nose, which according to his code of conduct signified genuine emotion. Naturally he was always prepared for sacrifices. But if even that was of no use, then they would have to . . .

Mrs Dewley crumpled and smoothed out her narrow envelope. Her shoulders shivered: she must have caught a cold, something which happens very easily in hot weather.

Around her the pink and blue ladies pecked and fluttered.

9

VERY WELL, SIR

Didi got up later than usual. It was after midday. She was humming a tune and combing out her unruly boyish curls in front of the mirror. She was wearing her favourite black pyjamas. The front of them was open to the waist and they were lightly held together by a cord. Beneath the black cord the pink of her flesh could be seen. In this costume and with her short hair—half girl, half boy—she was like a mediaeval page for whose sake virtuous ladies soon forgot their knights and so eagerly cast down rope ladders from the balconies of their towers.

In the next room Campbell tossed and turned heavily. Three days ago the room next to Didi's had become vacant. For three days he had been living there, or rather, had been flying somewhere in his bedevilled motor car, flying through whatever lay in his path, as if in a dream. Soon he would regain control and all this would end. He had only to earn another thirty pounds and then he would be able to rent one of the thousands of identical houses and once more the ground would be firm beneath his feet.

'Dearest Johnny,'—Didi was talking to her china pug—'you won't mind, will you, if I get just a teeny bit married? You know me, after all. Well then, you just be quiet and smile, and now . . .'

Someone knocked at number 72. It must be Nancy from the new revue.

'Nancy, come in.' The door creaked. Didi came out from behind the screen and saw the Reverend Dewley. His eyebrows leaped into an astonished triangle. With a snort of displeasure he stepped backwards towards the door into the corridor.

'I'm terribly sorry, I thought that since it was after twelve, most people . . .' And he seized the door handle, but Didi grasped it as well.

'No, no, please don't be embarrassed, for goodness sake. Do sit down. This is what I usually wear in the morning and it's a very fetching style, don't you think? I've heard so much about you. I'm very glad that at last you've . . .'

One simply had to sacrifice oneself utterly. The vicar sat down, trying not to look at her usual morning attire.

'You see, Miss . . . er, Didi . . . I have come on behalf of an unhappy mother. Of course, you can't understand what it means to have a child.'

'Oh but Mr Dewley, I do have one. This is my only Johnny and I love him terribly.'

Didi lifted the pug to Reverend Dewley's triangular brows. 'Isn't he sweet? Come on Johnny, smile! Kiss Mr Dewley. There, don't be afraid.'

Johnny pressed his cold, smiling lips to the vicar's and

either out of the unexpectedness of it, or out of his innate politeness, the vicar actually replied to Johnny's china kiss.

'Oh what a dear you are!' Didi was thrilled. But the vicar felt quite differently about it. He jumped up in indignation.

'I'll come and see you again, Miss, when you're not in quite such high spirits. I'm in no way disposed . . .'

'Oh but Mr Dewley, unfortunately I always seem to be in high spirits.'

'In that case . . .'

Mr Dewley made for the next room, for Campbell. Here the task was less thankless. Campbell heard out Mr Dewley's whole speech, frowned strenuously and nodded: yes, yes. It could not be otherwise in fact. The vicar's speech was extremely logical and he drew Campbell after him along the rails. The vicar was exultant. But at the last stop, the train unexpectedly crashed. Campbell leaped up from his chair:

'Mr Dewley, I would ask you not to express yourself in such terms about Didi, whom I have asked to be my wife.'

'Your w-wife?' But the vicar immediately recovered himself. 'But Mr Campbell, you've agreed with me all along, haven't you?'

'Yes, I have,' Campbell nodded gloomily.

'So, where's your sense of logic, Mr Campbell?'

'Logic?' Campbell frowned, wiped his brow and suddenly lowering his head like a bull, went for the vicar: 'Yes, my wife! I said my wife! Yes! And now if you'll excuse me, I want to be left alone.'

'So that's how it is. Very well, sir.' The vicar walked out, his eyebrows raised very high, which this time, according to his code, signified cold indignation.

10

THE ELECTRIC IRON

It was already June. The trees in the parks had unfortunately lost their respectable, well-clipped air. The oleanders were in flower, bursting out all over the place in complete disorder. At night, the birds poured out their song, completely disregarding the fact that respectable people had gone to bed at ten o'clock. The respectable people banged their windows and leaned out in their white night-caps.

However, it must be admitted that even in Jesmond there was an anarchic element. And this element wholeheartedly approved of what was happening. They contrived to avoid the park-keeper's watchful eye and after ten o'clock stayed in the bushes to listen to the birdsong. All night the bushes were intensely alive. They stirred and whispered, while all night the moon wandered above the park wearing a monocle and looked down with the benevolent irony of the china pug.

All this produced a sort of strange illness: the bushes, the heat, the moon, the oleanders, all at once. Didi was being capricious. It was not clear what she wanted. Campbell felt flustered.

'It's hot. I can't . . .' Didi undid another button of her blouse. And waves rolled evenly in front of Campbell's eyes—white ones made of cambric, then others which were pink, and still others, which were loud and red in Campbell's head.

Campbell tried to distract Didi with something interesting: 'You know, Didi, I saw an electric iron in a window on King Street yesterday. A splendid one and it only costs ten shillings. I think we might start to get some things for the house.'

But even to this Didi responded listlessly. Yes, she must be ill. She let down the blinds and lay on the bed.

'Look Campbell, I'm feverish. Feel here. I am, aren't I? No, further down—here . . .' She moved Campbell's hand.

And once more all of Campbell was concentrated in a few square inches of his hand. From somewhere far away he heard his blood pulsing with regular beats, bursting out, a minute more and . . .

But Campbell, thank goodness, once more had the wheels in his hands and was steering straight for the little house with the electric iron. He removed his hand.

'Yes, it looks like a fever. It's nothing. Just the weather.'

Johnny the pug on the mantelpiece and the moon in the monocle at the window smiled their identical smiles. Campbell got up angrily and turned Johnny's face to the wall.

'No, please don't, please don't! You'd better give him to me.' Didi stretched out her hand.

The moon plunged into the soft linen clouds, grew dim and then began grinning again. And in answer, Didi's face flickered and changed constantly. Her eyebrows drew together and then apart. She was thinking and thinking . . . What was there to think about now? All lay firmly and squarely ahead: the little house and the shining white doorstep and the green or blue vase for the Sunday carnations.

'Johnny, my dear little Johnny.' Didi embraced the china pug. 'Kiss me Johnny. That's it—again! Again!'

She kissed him and he became warm and alive. She smothered him in her scent, the bittersweet scent of stocks, which were dry from the lack of rain. She drowned Johnny's mocking face in the white and pink waves and called him strange names. But Campbell sat in silence, stubbornly thrusting out his stony chin at the moon and looking so like the portrait of the late Sir Harold.

Nowadays, O'Kelly rarely came round, but if he did come, then he was the same as ever: sleepy, unbuttoned, wicked, and jolly.

Campbell told him seriously, 'We've already got twenty pounds. We need another thirty pounds, and then for fifty we can buy all the furniture.'

'I suppose you can't possibly manage without furniture?' smirked O'Kelly.

'Oh no, of course not,' Campbell replied with imperturbable seriousness. 'There is absolutely nothing to laugh at. What's so funny about it? It's all quite logical.'

'But, my dear Campbell, you must apply your logic skilfully; otherwise, for all you know, it will crush you.'

And then, goodness knows why, O'Kelly told the story of his aunt Eva: in her old age her mind had seized up and she began to be afraid of drinking anything, in case she swallowed any germs. She did not swallow any germs; but she died of thirst very soon after.

Little by little, Didi began to listen and slowly unknit her brows. Slowly the laughing page woke up. Then O'Kelly walked up to the fireplace and picked up Johnny the pug.

'He really does look like me, eh? Looking at him, I could shave without a mirror.'

Her eyebrows relaxed completely. Didi laughed. 'That's simply brilliant, if you thought it up yourself. Well, confess, did you or not? Come on, won't you confess?' She shook O'Kelly. His head hung helplessly as packages fell out of his pockets.

'Aha, pistachios? Oysters? Is there champagne?'

Well, of course there was. A merry picnic began on the green carpet. O'Kelly swallowed an oyster and sank his teeth into the English. Oh, these English!

'As righteous as oysters and as serious as wellington boots. My God, the English! I'd take the lot of them and squeeze some lemon juice on to them, like this . . . just like this. Aha? So you've stirred?'

The door was opening quietly and Nancy appeared. She was half Irish and so O'Kelly greeted her particularly warmly. And besides, she was . . .

Nancy was dressed only in a pale pink blouse and carried a turkish towel on her arm. With a most naive air, she walked round the room and warned them, 'Please don't come out into the corridor: I'm going to have a bath.'

This was splendid. Even Campbell laughed. But he laughed in his own way. When everyone else had stopped, only he remembered and filled again with laughter. The heavy lorry rushed forward and simply would not stop.

Wrapping herself in the towel, Nancy graciously agreed to take part in the picnic before having her bath. O'Kelly bubbled and overflowed. Didi shook her short curls—the mischievous boy pursed her lips, showing how the Reverend Dewley kissed the pug. And again, everyone had forgotten, had fallen silent, but Campbell remembered and burst out laughing. And even when he was alone in his room, and everyone had gone, he remembered again, and started laughing.

Everything was quiet. It was a close night. It was difficult to breathe. It smothered you from the head down, like a quilt. No, it was impossible to go to sleep. Didi took the cold pug from the chest of drawers. She kissed him until he became warm and alive. But Campbell dreamed of an electric iron: huge and shining, it crept along and ironed everything until nothing remained. No houses, no trees—only something as flat and smooth as a mirror.

Campbell looked on in admiration, thinking, 'And all for ten shillings!'

II

TOO HOT

The Reverend Dewley never missed an opportunity of instilling his *Precepts* into the Jesmond consciousness. On Saturday, he spoke at the Salvation Army meeting. If the government wishes to wallow in its stubbornness and neglect its duties, then it is up to each one of us to drive our neighbours along the road to salvation, as you would drive scorpions, or slaves. Better they be slaves of God than free sons of Satan.

The speech had a tremendous effect and the Jesmond branch of the Salvation Army decided to take up the matter immediately the very next day.

It was Sunday—bright, sunny and hot. At half past eight in the morning the Salvation Army set off from their headquarters. Waving banners, singing hymns and beating a drum, the two hundred soldiers of the Salvation Army walked through the town at a steady march. A tall severe woman officer in a blue bonnet stopped at every door and knocked.

'Christ the Lord is calling you to church!'

'Hello! Christ the Lord is calling you . . . Hello, hello!'

She knocked until the people inside woke up and astonished faces began to look out. On that day the church of St Enoch was full. The vicar returned home happy and exhausted. The secretary of the Honourable Society of Bell-ringers, MacIntosh, followed him respectfully shaking his head in admiration: what eloquence, what unflagging energy!

'And so, my dear MacIntosh, today it's your turn,' said the vicar as he took his leave. 'It may be difficult, but it is a duty you must perform.'

Mr MacIntosh set out for a walk. He did not choose a very picturesque place for his walk—the street where Mrs Aunty's furnished rooms were situated. Apparently strange ideas sometimes entered his head.

The vicar, having lunched, sat down in an armchair. It was very hot. Dozens of little reflected suns poured through the patterned panes at the top of the windows. The vicar admired them: convenient, pocket-sized suns that were not too bright. As he was sitting there, he dozed off: this was part of the Sunday timetable. Even when asleep, his face retained its polite, refined expression; everything was at the ready, so that at any moment he could open his eyes and say: splendid weather, isn't it?

The Salvation Army did not of course forget Mrs Aunty's furnished rooms for artistes, alarming the inhabitants at an unearthly hour. Consequently, the inhabitants had not slept enough. They banged the door and splashed in the bath louder than was necessary.

Didi came into lunch frowning. She studied Campbell with astonishment, as if seeing him for the first time, although he was the same as ever: huge, solid and unshakeable. So as to earn the remaining thirty pounds the sooner, Campbell had taken on private work at home. Immediately after coffee, he undid his cuffs and went to his room to work.

Knitting her brows, Didi sat next to him and stroked the pug. The sun rose higher and knocked importunately at the window. Campbell got up and lowered the blinds.

'But I want the sun.' Didi leaped up.

'But my dear, you know that I'm working so that we can begin buying the furniture sooner and then . . .'

Didi suddenly burst out laughing without letting him finish and went off to her room. She put the pug on the mantelpiece and looked into his charmingly ugly face.

'What do you think, Johnny?'

Clearly Johnny was thinking the same thing. Didi hurriedly pinned on her hat.

Ten minutes later, excited by the dazzling success of his walk, MacIntosh stood in front of Mrs Dewley. 'We must go to Sandy Bay,' he said, mysteriously emphasising the word 'must'.

For a moment, Mrs Dewley's pince-nez ceased to be of crystal, but flashed with fire. 'You're quite sure?'

Mr MacIntosh simply shrugged his shoulders with an offended air and looked at his watch.

'We have seven minutes until the train leaves.'

In her haste, Mrs Dewley's sleeve caught against her pince-nez, which fell to the floor. Mrs Dewley fixed them more firmly and once again she was Mrs Dewley. Now they could go.

There was no escape from the sun. At Sandy Bay it was blinding and made your blood boil. The white foaming surf seethed and throbbed. O'Kelly and Didi lay on the hot sand. Didi's temples pulsated and O'Kelly had difficulty in finding his words—probably because of the sun.

'It's too hot. Let's go for a swim,' Didi got up. The sand was pale from the intense heat. The waves were sparkling jasper-green with frothy white crests. Heads in orange, pink and violet caps bobbed on the waves. The sun and the laughter were muffled by the waves.

The water was refreshing; it was hard to get out. Didi said to herself, 'We're just having a swim and then we'll go straight home.'

The waves carried them further and further. They dashed along and caught them, spinning them round, and it was so good not to struggle, not to think, to submit. Only O'Kelly's head was visible above the water—the ugly grinning face of the pug. He called out something which was hard to catch above the noise of the waves.

'. . . all night . . . agreed?'

Didi—had she heard him?—nodded her head.

When they went into a café to eat after their swim, O'Kelly saw Mrs Dewley at one of the tables, and with her MacIntosh's profound football head. O'Kelly ran up to them.

'What's brought you here? Mrs Dewley, I'm so pleased that you are not yet completely petrified.'

'Petrified?'

'Yes, I was just telling . . . my young lady. In a few years, the curious traveller to England will find only petrified, immobile people, made of limestone, and limestone trees, dogs and clouds . . . if there hasn't been an earthquake by then, or something like that.'

Mrs Dewley's pince-nez glittered coldly. She was looking with an ironic smile at a strange package with a handle, which O'Kelly was waving vigorously.

'That must be your famous inflatable suitcase, Mr O'Kelly.'

For a split second O'Kelly was slightly embarrassed.

'Oh, you know a good hunter never goes anywhere without his gun. It's just a habit. Are you getting the five o'clock? I hope we'll meet on the train, if I'm not late.'

'I should be delighted.' The lenses of Mrs Dewley's pince-nez sparkled.

O'Kelly's unpunctuality was well-known: and of course he missed the five o'clock train.

12

THE BIRTH OF CAMPBELL

The heat lessened suddenly and a damp, milky mist fell. In the night the distinct and unceasing sound of drops of water splashing against the window-sill was particularly clear, like a clock marking off time until an appointed hour.

And when this hour came—it just happened to be on Campbell's birthday—a letter was received in a narrow ice-blue envelope. The letter was unsigned:

'Dear Sir, being your friends, we cannot but inform you that your acquaintances, Mr O'K. and Miss D., are abusing your trust; you will have an opportunity of convincing yourself of this beyond doubt.'

The narrow blue envelope was somehow familiar. Thinking about it, Campbell remembered. It was quite clear that this was utter invention. Campbell was absolutely positive.

But all the same, when he went to the office he didn't feel quite himself: it was as if he had drunk a cup of tea and seen a fly at the bottom. He had thrown the fly out, but all the same . . . Maybe it was just the mist: the air was close, like cotton-wool, and your footsteps sounded strangely muffled, as if someone was continuously walking behind you.

In the office, O'Kelly met Campbell noisily and merrily: he was more noisy and colourful than ever. It turned out that O'Kelly had not forgotten that today was not just any day, but Campbell's birthday and he had prepared some sort of present for Campbell. What kind it was, would only be revealed that evening. Then, smiling like an Easter lamb, Cecily brought Campbell a bouquet of white lilies. Campbell was very touched.

And when he got home, yet another present was waiting for him: Didi herself—herself!—suggested that they went to the shops and began to buy those things. Campbell's fly disappeared without trace.

'The iron,' Campbell beamed, 'no, first the iron, and then . . .'

'The iron's heavy, we ought to get it when we've finished, rather than drag it round all the time,' Didi argued reasonably.

But Campbell insisted. They bought the iron and Campbell carried it gladly. It was not at all heavy, honestly: it was as light as a feather.

The lights were lit. The mist was thickening. It was Campbell's birthday—the day of his real birth, the beginning of a new life. And Jesmond seemed new in the mist, an unfamiliar town he had not seen before. Their footsteps rang out unusually cheerfully, as if someone was walking persistently behind them.

And Campbell also desperately wanted to buy some underwear for Didi. Didi refused, but Campbell would not listen. Today was his birthday.

'For your wife?'

'No, not exactly,' Campbell smiled with embarrassment at the assistant.

Chemises and drawers made of transparent silk—her body would glow gently pink through them. There was a kind of joyful shame in turning them over and examining them all, with her, with Didi. With every new thing that he bought for her, she became more and more his wife. Campbell's ears were burning and he noticed that Didi was hiding her face.

Campbell laughed. 'Come on, Didi, be brave: look at me.'

He wanted to see the same sweet shame on her face. But Didi would not show it.

In the evening, O'Kelly appeared with a heap of packages, accompanied by Cecily.

'It'll be like Noah's Ark,' O'Kelly explained. He turned to the fireplace and threw open his arms. The shining iron stood in splendour on the mantelpiece next to Johnny the pug.

'Next to Johnny?' He looked at Didi with reproach. Then he turned to Campbell. 'And so it's all settled: "I'm yours for ever", isn't that right, Campbell? As for me, I'm just plain stupid. I could never understand how it's possible to love one and the same woman every day, how one could read the same book every day. In the end, you're bound to turn out semi-literate.'

The champagne had a strange effect on Didi that day. She sat by the table and tore sheets of writing paper out of the pad and with great pleasure ripped them into little pieces.

Cecily was flushed from the wind and was struggling with O'Kelly over her fourth button. She allowed him to undo three buttons of her blouse, but the fourth ...

'No, it's not decent,' Cecily answered with the grave and innocent expression of an Easter lamb.

'But why is the fourth one particularly indecent?' laughed O'Kelly. 'Why were three allowed?'

Didi was still tearing the paper. O'Kelly took the pad away from her and asked for silence. The main thing he wanted to draw his listeners' attention to was the lined writing paper. They don't write letters on any other sort of paper in Jesmond. And this is quite correct, seeing as these lines are the very rails along which thought in Jesmond must travel, in accordance with the strictest timetable. The wisdom of life lies in figures and that is why he welcomed his adored Cecily's three-button morality. And seeing as he, O'Kelly, and no one else, was the Serpent who had tempted Campbell to go off the rails of the parish of St Enoch ... O'Kelly took out a cheque for fifty pounds and held it out to Campbell:

'So that you can go out tomorrow and buy the rest of your irons ...'

And as Campbell hesitated, O'Kelly added: 'It's a loan, of course. And I demand that you write me an IOU today, this very minute. Well?'

Campbell's head was spinning—it meant that the very next day ... Campbell's hands and voice shook. 'I can't speak like you, O'Kelly. But you understand ... you're my only friend, the only one who ...'

At this point, Didi burst out laughing quite absurdly. Louder and more shrilly she laughed, out of control, and exclaimed through her tears: 'Don't you dare to take it, Campbell! Don't you dare to take money from him. Don't you dare, I won't have it.'

However, she soon calmed down and grew quieter. Doubtless it was just one of her tantrums—there was no other reason. Didi couldn't say herself why she should not want him to take it.

'You see, it's your champagne,' said Campbell with fond reproach to Mr O'Kelly.

O'Kelly left with Cecily, the Easter lamb, on his arm.

Campbell's birthday was over and tomorrow a new life was beginning. Tomorrow he would look for a little house.

13

ADVENTURES IN THE MIST

Didi had promised to go and see Mr O'Kelly again after the performance and O'Kelly ran round all the florists trying to find Easter lilies. Didi was mad about them—the strange, china-white bloom made of one huge carelessly folded petal, with its protruding, sting-like stamen, and its dry, sweet, languid scent. In the asymmetry of the bloom, and the contrast between the china-whiteness and the scent, there was something irritating, rather like O'Kelly's way of speaking. In a word, Didi liked Easter lilies and he must get hold of some at any cost. The season for them was already over, and it was only on King Street that O'Kelly was lucky enough to find the last ones, beginning to wilt, made of old yellowing china.

With the bunch under his arm, he ran out of the shop whistling. His thoughts were bubbling merrily like champagne. And out of the sparkling foam, Didi emerged like Venus, in her black pyjamas.

'A Venus of today ought to appear like that, though—in pyjamas. Nudity is just too virtuous . . .' reflected O'Kelly, whistling.

'Good evening, my dear Mr O'Kelly. Splendid weather, isn't it?'

O'Kelly nearly tripped up. In front of him shone Mr Dewley's golden teeth.

'Doubtless you're on the way to your office,' said Dewley, with a barely perceptible smile.

'Why should I be going to my office?' O'Kelly was slightly

embarrassed. Nobody knew what was going on at the office in the evenings and it was very odd that Dewley should . . . 'I'm not such an ass as to work in the evenings as well,' O'Kelly laughed without constraint.

'Ah, I see. In that case . . .' Dewley lifted his plate-shaped minister's hat. And O'Kelly rolled on merrily once more, holding the bunch of flowers under his arm. When O'Kelly turned into the High Street, it was already getting dark. Street-lamps had been lit and were flickering in the countless crevices of the narrow alleyways between the old houses. A mist wafted up from the river. Everything lost its everyday appearance and it was easier to live, easier to deceive. Iron clanged in a smithy. A reddish smoke came from the street-lamps. And one could believe that down below by the river, Oliver Cromwell's horsemen were gathered round a bonfire. And that this black figure was the handsome and unfortunate Rizzio, stealing past to Mary Stuart. O'Kelly was deep in thought and stood with his hands thrust in his pockets. But Rizzio turned round, and O'Kelly thought he saw that he was wearing a minister's flat hat. What sort of strange meeting was this? Or was it all just the mist? O'Kelly pressed himself up against the window of an antique shop and examined minutely the bronze door-knocker in the shape of an ugly head—half man, half dog—which had turned green. Then he cautiously ran across to the other side of the street and followed Rizzio. Yes, it was him: a cardboard figure, his hands carefully folded behind his back and his fingers counting something. It was Dewley. And Cobbler John's Alley was rather an odd place for a vicar to take a walk.

O'Kelly dived into the nearest passageway, ran down to the river along the dark crack between the high walls, then through the back streets, and came out again on to King Street. When he had wandered round the streets for an hour, O'Kelly found himself once more in front of Cobbler John's Alley. The mist had settled and you could see clearly that there was no one around. O'Kelly went into the building by the iron-plated side door. Adjoining O'Kelly's office was a small vaulted room with a window looking out on to the alley, an old narrow window, a loophole with a grill across it. This room was unrecognisable now: old faded tapestries on the walls, two wrought-iron lamps bought from the antique shop opposite. A very low Turkish divan about a foot off the floor ran along an entire wall. The flames played subtly in the grate and Didi looked so cosy by the fire, in her black pyjamas.

Just to lie there—transfixed by the golden play of the fire, to sip the sharp golden wine and to half listen to O'Kelly's sharp words.

'... My dear girl, it's just what I want, for you to be unhappy after you've settled in with Campbell and his irons. Happiness is one of the most fattening conditions. But you ought to remain exactly the same: slim, short-haired, half-girl and half-boy ...'

O'Kelly's hand stroked her so gently and somewhere far away Didi wearily saw the oddly contradictory Easter lilies and heard her own voice: 'But it's so cruel to deceive Campbell. He's just a big child.'

'Cruel,' O'Kelly laughed, 'it's cruel to tell children the truth. If anything convinces me of God's mercy, then it's his gift of making us able to lie.'

O'Kelly didn't finish. It sounded as though a key was being turned in the lock of the side door into Cobbler John's Alley and that there were someone's footsteps upon the stone staircase. However, O'Kelly clearly remembered locking the door with the key—it was just Cobbler John's ghost wandering through the old building.

'I wouldn't be surprised if old John walked in here.' O'Kelly stretched out. 'The mist has made everything seem so fantastical today.'

Didi had left for the theatre and told Campbell that she had to go and see someone afterwards. Campbell sat alone without lighting the fire. The drops of rain tapped against the window regularly and distinctly, like a clock ticking. When it had grown quite dark, old Mrs Taylor brought a letter from Lady Campbell. Lady Campbell asked her son to come round that evening without fail. Clearly this was at last the long-awaited reconciliation. Things had turned out even better than he could have hoped. Campbell dressed quickly and set out.

It was obvious that Lady Campbell wished to arrange the ratification of the peace treaty with all due ceremony. The dining-room was brightly lit, and around the table Campbell saw Mrs Dewley, the Reverend Dewley rubbing his hands and the football-headed MacIntosh. Campbell approached Lady Campbell joyfully, but the invisible bridle pulled her head even higher, and with an imperious gesture she sternly pointed Campbell to a seat.

'Sit down.' She paused and raised her eyes up to the portrait of Sir Harold in his wig and robes. 'My God, what would your late father, Sir Harold, have said?'

She could say no more: the vicar spoke for her. Who else could say everything which needed to be said?

'My dear Mr Campbell. We have asked you here because we love you, for Christ taught us that we should love even sinners. We are obliged to resort to extreme measures in order to lead you back on to the path of righteousness. Now you will follow me and Mr MacIntosh . . .' And noticing that Campbell wished to object, the vicar added: 'If only for your mother's sake, just look at her.'

Lady Campbell gazed piously at the portrait of the late Sir Harold and two meagre tears appeared in her eyes. This was the most she could allow herself without offending propriety. Next to her sat Mrs Dewley, shaking feverishly, her eyes downcast. Campbell spoke calmly, 'Very well, let's go.' All this was of course the same kind of vile joke as the letter in the blue envelope and it was necessary to have done with it once and for all.

The streets were empty. The wind was blowing from the river once more, driving the mist, shrouding the roofs. And the walls of the buildings rose right up into the skies. They walked in silence along the crack between the walls. Gradually Campbell understood that they were going to

O'Kelly's office. The crack was continually moving in, pressing down on him, and there was nothing in the world except the walls rising up to the skies. There was no escaping from the walls: on and on between the walls, as if in a dream. And as in a dream, he knew without knowing what awaited him at the end of his journey. They stopped in Cobbler John's Alley in front of the plated door. A light shone through the narrow loophole above them.

'Well, sir.' Rubbing his hands triumphantly, the vicar looked at Campbell. Campbell knocked at the plated door like a blind man.

'It's locked.' He turned helplessly. His stubborn, square chin twitched.

'Don't worry, we've got hold of a key.' The football head popped out of the mist. It was a huge awkward key. 'These skeleton keys really are an education. You can't beat them,' MacIntosh added.

They heard Campbell take two steps up the stone staircase and then he stopped. For a moment it was quiet. Then the footsteps lumbered up the staircase, turning into a clatter—Campbell was running upstairs. Then the upper door banged. There was a moment's silence and then Campbell was already lumbering down again. With a roar, Campbell rushed downwards past the vicar, not looking where he was going, like a huge bedevilled lorry with no steering.

14

THE WATERMAN PEN

In the morning Campbell, as always, shaved carefully and put on a clean collar. When he looked in the mirror he noticed with astonishment that he was exactly the same as always. Except that his little elephantine eyes had grown a bit bigger and a dark shadow had crept under them during the night. In the dining-room, Campbell picked up the paper and mechanically began to look at the advertisements for houses to let, as he had been doing for the last few days. He caught himself doing it, smiled, and put the paper aside. He drank his usual two cups of coffee. He began buttering some bread, but for some reason did not eat it, placing it carefully on the plate instead. And it was only when he noticed that he had a whole mound of bread in front of him that he felt embarrassed and left the table.

It was already time to go to the office, but Campbell went back into his bedroom. He locked himself in to think it all over again from the very beginning and come to a decision. But all the wheels in his head had ground to a halt and in the place of any thought he saw only one thing—the painfully clear pink and black lacing on *her* chest and *his* funny thin bandy legs.

When the bell rang for lunch, Campbell came to and understood that there was absolutely nothing to think about. Everything had already been decided by someone else, and now he was walking between stone walls, which reached up to the skies. There was no turning off. He could only walk forwards, on to the end.

Campbell opened the drawer of the table and took out an old revolver with needle-shaped bullets, left to him by his father. Then he wrote a cheque to Lady Campbell for the thirty pounds which he still had in the bank and tore up O'Kelly's cheque for fifty pounds. At this point he noticed that the pen he was writing with belonged to O'Kelly. Obviously O'Kelly had left it there on Campbell's birthday. It was an ordinary Waterman fountain pen and now of course he must give it back to him.

Campbell frowned painfully: everything else was clear and simple, but this business with the Waterman was terribly difficult. He had to give it back, and so would have to say something to him. All this complicated the position. Campbell put the pen in the same pocket of his jacket as the revolver. All the way there he thought about the pen: how could he actually . . .

And so, looking worried and frowning, he walked into

O'Kelly's office. O'Kelly was sitting in his office with his papers, just the same as yesterday, but nonetheless there was something completely different about him. Staring for a moment, Campbell noticed that O'Kelly was not smiling. This was as unbelievable as the idea of Johnny the china pug suddenly ceasing to smile. It simply wasn't O'Kelly. Looking perplexed, Campbell put his hand in his pocket, took out the Waterman and put it on the table.

'Here. Your pen . . . you forgot it. I have to return it to you.'

O'Kelly opened his eyes wide in amazement and looked from the Waterman to the perplexed Campbell and from Campbell to the pen. Then he turned red as for a minute he filled with laughter and then burst out, 'My God. My Waterman. Campbell, you're . . . you're . . . inimitable.'

Now he was the same as ever, he was O'Kelly. Without hesitating, Campbell pulled out the revolver and fired somewhere three times. O'Kelly slowly slumped forward until his head was buried in the papers. Campbell heard neither O'Kelly's cries, nor those of his four wives. He put on his hat, walked out and felt terribly tired. He had never felt so tired in his life.

In the High Street he went up to a policeman who was dozing peacefully, and said, 'I have just killed Mr O'Kelly the lawyer. Please be quick and take me where you have to. I'm so tired.'

The policeman gaped. His whole body and his eyes like saucers were so clearly thinking 'madman', that Campbell added, 'Well, go and ask in the office and I'll wait. Only please hurry.'

A minute later, Campbell and the policeman were walking together down Cobbler John's Alley. They walked silently between the smooth walls rising up to the skies and through the mist Campbell remembered that at some time he had already walked endlessly between two smooth endless walls . . .

15

THE GREYISH-WHITE SCALES

The autumn wind whipped itself up, raged and whistled. A huge grey bird bore in from the sea, covering half the sky with its wings, looming nearer and nearer, slow, silent, relentless, and it grew darker all the time. But the crowd did not disperse: there was a rumour that the murderer might be pardoned. Indeed, the name and work of his father, the late Sir Harold, were still not forgotten and it might well turn out that . . .

'Down with the gentry!' croaked someone stubbornly and hoarsely. 'A year ago they'd have strung this gunman up alive . . . Down with the gentry!'

The lamp by the entrance to the prison jerked and swayed and the white walls shook, ready to collapse. Justice was in danger. The football head of Mr MacIntosh emerged from the crowd. He was agitated and his voice trembled.

'Gentlemen, justice and civilisation are inseparable. We must come to the defence of civilisation. Gentlemen, can one imagine anything more savage than a deliberate and premeditated murder? And therefore, unfortunately, yes, I tell you, unfortunately we must demand execution.'

'Down with the gentry!'

The wind howled. The lamp cast a long band of light, and in it faces, bowlers, collars shimmered like the bright scales of a snake writhing with a slow endless movement. It was impossible to make out their words: the snake shimmered and hissed.

From somewhere a crowd of boys rushed past as if they had been let out of a cage, all barefoot and all wearing white collars.

'*Jesmond Star*! Extra, extra! Lawyer O'Kelly's murderer pardoned!'

'What, already? Pardoned?' Everyone seized the white sheets. But it was only a matter of a possible pardon. The report added that taking into account the work of the late Sir

Harold, it would be more than . . .

'Down with the gentry!'

'Gentlemen, justice . . .'

'Down with the *Jesmond Star*!'

The greyish-white scales still shimmered more under the lamp. The snake rustled along the asphalt, wriggled to the offices of the *Jesmond Star* and spread itself out into twenty coils in front of the dark windows. There was no one in the offices. A stone rang against the glass. The splinters tinkled and scattered. But the windows remained just as empty and dark. And the dark silent bird above loomed very close.

It was time to go home. The pink and blue wives were already waiting patiently in their beds. They were waiting to ask, their faces contorted with fear and curiosity: 'Surely they won't pardon him? Surely not . . .'

And then they shuddered and embraced their husbands ardently. How good it was to be alive!

Towards night the wind unexpectedly dropped and it grew tranquil and black as if the whole world had vanished somewhere. Sometimes a distracted man dashes about all day, starts at the sound of a bell and laughs with a terrifying laugh; while his eyes sink deeper and deeper and he has only one thought: to bury his head in the pillow, to vanish into the blackness, to fall asleep. And it was this sort of night: day had buried its head in the black pillow and disappeared . . . not a glimmer, not a murmur.

Towards night Mrs Dewley felt somehow easier. All day she had felt very strange: her pince-nez had disappeared again, and all day she wandered around as if she was blind, stumbling and bumping into people. She seemed to keep running off to buy things, and when she got to the shops she didn't need to buy anything. And anyway that was not the point. The point was that she didn't care. Why should she buy anything now?

Dinner was at a quarter past six instead of six o'clock and the vicar raised his eyebrows into a sharp triangle.

'My dear, surely it's so simple to keep a spare pair. And

then you wouldn't have this strange look about you. And we'd have some sort of order. And you know . . .'

'Very well, I'll buy them tomorrow.' Mrs Dewley shuddered and corrected herself. 'The day after tomorrow.'

Because tomorrow who in the world could buy anything? Tomorrow, on the day when there in the prison, they would lead Campbell out into the courtyard and put the . . .

It was dark in the bedroom. One didn't have to look at anything. Maybe this was why Mrs Dewley felt easier and she unexpectedly fell asleep. She probably only slept for a few minutes. Then she awoke, opened her eyes and saw the vicar's white flannel night-cap. The vicar, in accordance with what was prescribed in the *Precepts*, lay with his arms folded on his chest, peacefully snoring. All was black and tranquil. The whole world had vanished. If you howled and cried no one would hear you or do anything. The world was sleeping peacefully, snoring in a flannel night-cap.

Nobody knows how long the vicar was asleep, because he only woke up at Mrs Dewley's howling. Immediately he realised, 'It's a nightmare. Better wake her up.' You could not include dreams in a timetable. The vicar was very frightened of dreams. Mrs Dewley must have been sleeping very soundly. She cried out louder and louder and only grew quiet when he seized her by the shoulder with a cold hand.

'I don't think you ought to have supper at night, my dear.'

'No, I don't think I should,' Mrs Dewley answered in the darkness. Five minutes later the vicar was asleep once more, snoring peacefully. All was black and tranquil.

16

THE TRIUMPHANT SUN

It was to take place at half past nine, which was just as it should be. Every well-bred man must have time to shave and breakfast. The fact that it was to take place at half past nine only showed the respect of one well-bred man towards another—even if he was a criminal. The sun was very bright. The sun was triumphant. This was clear to everyone and the only question was whether it was celebrating the victory of justice, and consequently of civilisation—or whether . . .

The greyish-white scales rustled and shimmered anxiously.

'Look here, gentlemen, hasn't anything been heard yet?'

No, nothing had reached them yesterday, but maybe this morning . . . In the end, everything would be decided by the last minute. Would the prison bell toll at half past nine or not?

Making his way to the prison was a neatly shaven, pink old man, of the kind that have a tasty look, like rich, well-browned pies. The old man knocked and the iron-plated door set in the prison wall opened before him.

Mrs Dewley turned to the vicar. Her breath came short and quick.

'Who . . . who was that? Who's that just went in?'

'Who? Him? That, my dear, is a master of his trade.'

Mrs Dewley seized the vicar by the arms and held on to him for dear life. 'You . . . you mean to say that that's the man who will have to . . .'

The vicar shook her hands away. 'People can s-s-see you. I don't have anything to s-s-say. You don't know how to control yours-s-self.'

Mrs Dewley fell silent. A nearby clock caught her eye. 'Two minutes to half past nine.'

Two minutes. The scales tightened, froze, and remained motionless. Frequenters of boxing matches and the races, with faces as red as beefsteaks, could not take their eyes off the clock. The brass of the Salvation Army band shone indifferently. The ruddy, tipsy sun rolled out triumphantly. The frost on the roof melted and dripped, like a clock distinctly marking the seconds until half past nine. And then it dripped once more, the last drop: half past. There was a tense moment, brittle as glass, and . . . nothing happened. The bell was silent. Immediately the scales stirred and rumbled, louder and louder. Everyone felt insulted: the boxing and racing fans and the upholders of civilisation. They seethed and writhed. They waved their arms. The coils wound and unwound malevolently. They were still waiting for something and did not disperse.

Mrs Dewley, without her pince-nez, her hat askew, seized the vicar by the arms again.

'Do you . . . do you understand? This means that he . . . It means they won't . . . Do you understand?'

The Reverend Dewley was not listening. He was watching the clock: it was already twenty to ten. At a quarter to ten, when there was no longer any reason to expect anything, the prison bell suddenly sang out in its slow bronze voice: a measured bronze drop, falling from the sky.

Mrs Dewley shrieked in a strange voice—not a Jesmond voice—'No, no, for God's sake! Stop! Sto . . .'

Nothing more could be heard. The scales of the snake spun furiously. The air was bright with handkerchiefs and cheers. The sun shone triumphantly, rosy and indifferent. The Salvation Army band played a drawling hymn. People fell to their knees with relief, to pray for the soul of the murderer.

And then when all had quietened down, Reverend Dewley made a speech on the necessity of making the *Precepts of Salvation* part of one's life. After all, wasn't everything that had happened to disturb the peaceful flow of life in Jesmond the most convincing argument? If the government forcibly led weak souls along the only true path, it would not be necessary to resort to such sad, albeit just measures . . . Salvation would be mathematically inevitable, mathematically, you understand.

Everyone cheered the Reverend Dewley, the pride of Jesmond, and unanimously carried a resolution. Let us hope that this time the Bill on Compulsory Salvation will at last get through.

THE FISHER OF MEN

I

The most wonderful thing in life is to be delirious and the most wonderful kind of delirium is being in love. In the morning mist, hazy and amorous, London was delirious. London squinted as it floated along, milky-pink, without caring where it was going.

Yesterday the slender columns of the druid temples had still been factory chimneys. The airy iron arches of the viaducts were now bridges from one mysterious island to another. The black cranes, like huge prehistoric swans, stretched out their necks, about to dive to the bottom for prey. Frightened, the brazen gold letters: 'Rolls-Royce Automobiles' flashed up at the sun and faded out. Once more forming a hushed, hazy circle: the lace of the sinking towers, the swaying web of cables, the slow dance of the slumbering tortoise-houses. And as the fixed axis of it all—the gigantic stone phallus of Nelson's column.

At the bottom of the milky-pink sea, Bailey the organist floated along the empty morning streets, without caring where he was going. He shuffled along the asphalt, getting his absurdly long feet entangled. He screwed up his eyes blissfully and, thrusting his hands into his pockets, he stopped in front of the shop windows.

Here were shoes. Brown leggings, enormous black wellingtons and tiny patent leather shoes for ladies.

'Great craftsman of shoes, divine poet of shoes . . .' Bailey the organist prayed before the shoemaker's window, 'Thank you for the tiny shoes . . . and for the chimneys and the bridges and Rolls-Royce and the mist and springtime. And if it's painful—for the pain too . . .'

On the back of a sleepy elephant—the first morning bus—Bailey the organist hurried home to Chiswick. The conductress, broad and motherly, like a bun (at home she had a heap of children), was keeping a benevolent eye on the passenger. Looks like he has been drinking, poor devil. There, his lips have fallen open.

The fat lips, which must have been as soft as a foal's, smiled blissfully. His head, with its comfortable ears, which stuck out and curled up at the edges, swayed slightly. Bailey the organist was floating.

'Hey, sir, isn't this your stop?'

The organist opened his eyes wide in surprise. What, already?

'Had a drop to drink have we, sir?'

The foal's lips opened. The organist shook his head and laughed happily. 'Drink? My dear lady, better than that!'

He started down the stairs of the bus. Below in the mist, the Craggs' window, washed for Sunday, squinted with embarrassment and shone with milky-pink lights. The sun was rising.

The organist turned to the conductress, silently pointed the windows out to her, and just as silently embraced and kissed her with his soft foal's lips. The conductress wiped her mouth with her sleeve, burst out laughing and rang the bell: what can you expect from someone like that?

The organist dived into an alleyway, quietly unlocked the back gate of his house and went into the yard. He stopped by the coal pile and looked up over the brick wall at the window of his neighbours, the Craggs. In the window a white curtain breathed evenly in the wind. His neighbours were still asleep.

Taking off his hat, he stood there until a faint shadow flitted across the curtain. It flitted across and a hand shone pink in the sun as it lifted the edge. Bailey the organist put on his hat and went into his house.

2

Mr and Mrs Craggs were having breakfast. Everything in the room shone like metal: the fire irons, the mahogany chairs and the snow-white tablecloth. Perhaps the folds of the tablecloth were as rigid as metal and perhaps the chairs were as cold as metal to the touch—metal painted to look like mahogany.

On the uniformly green carpet behind Mr Craggs' metal chair were four light marks where the chair would be placed when breakfast had ended. And there were four light marks behind Mrs Craggs' chair as well.

On Sundays Mr Craggs allowed himself crab for breakfast. Mr Craggs adored crab. Swallowing bits of crab claw along with bits of his words, Mr Craggs was reading the newspaper aloud.

'The ship . . . mmm . . . lay keel up for a long time . . . people inside were hammering at the bottom of the ship . . . No, this is splendid crab, simply splendid! Zeppelins again over Kent, six men and eleven . . . mmm . . . eleven, yes, eleven women . . . To them people are just . . . just . . . Laurie, wouldn't you like a bit of crab?'

But Mrs Craggs had already finished her breakfast and was putting away the spoons. Mrs Craggs had a superb collection of teaspoons, a present from Craggs. They were silver spoons and each one was decorated in gilt and enamel with the arms of a town of the United Kingdom. Each spoon had its own little box. Mrs Craggs put the spoons away into their appropriate boxes and smiled. Across her lips hung a curtain of the lightest, but still opaque, pink silk. If you pulled the cord, it would immediately open wide and you would see what she was like behind the curtain: the real Laurie. But the cord was lost and the curtain only stirred faintly to and fro in the wind.

Mr Craggs, who had disappeared, suddenly rose up off the floor, positioned himself in front of Mrs Craggs on an invisible pedestal—a little iron monument—and held up a box. 'This is for you, my dear.'

In the box lay white and delicate pink underwear, something unbelievably lacy and stockings as fine as a spiderweb. Mr Craggs was a man of chaste views who could not stand nakedness, and his passion for lacy things was only the natural outcome of these chaste views.

Mrs Craggs was still not used to luxury. Mrs Craggs blushed and the pink curtain on her lips fluttered more quickly:

'Ah, you had some luck again . . . at the Stock Exchange, or . . . wherever it is you do your business, who can tell . . .'

'Hmm . . .' Mr Craggs sucked at his pipe and, as usual without lifting his iron eyelids, smiled triumphantly from his pedestal.

Mrs Craggs examined the delicate pink, the unbelievable laciness and the spiderweb. She discovered a seam had come unstitched on one pair of stockings and putting them aside, she offered her cheek to Mr Craggs. Craggs put out his pipe with his finger, put it into a pocket and planted his lips against her cheek. Mr Craggs' jaw and lips were thrust forward like a promontory into the sea of the world. They were lips made especially for sucking.

Mr Craggs sucked. A dusty ray of light beat against the window. Everything shone like metal.

3

Upstairs in the bedroom Mrs Craggs was once more looking over the stockings with the unstitched seam. She put everything away in the proper drawer of the chest. She washed her face meticulously with soap, took Mr Craggs' new trousers out of the wardrobe, and hung them up. He would be going to church in them.

The wind blew through the window. The trousers swayed. Doubtless, when they were on Mr Craggs, the trousers looked splendid and went perfectly well together with his body. But like this, isolated in space, Mr Craggs' trousers were nightmarish.

The wind blew through the window. As they swayed, the trousers were alive. A short, truncated, square creature consisting entirely of legs, belly and what went with them. And now it would get down and start walking among people and over people and grow and . . .

She must close the window. Mrs Craggs walked up to it and put her head out for a moment. Then she blushed slowly and deeply and angrily furrowed her brows: what, again?

Once more, in the yard to the right, by the coal pile, stood Bailey, the absurdly long and thin organist—a cardboard cut-out. He was holding his hat in his hands. The sun shone through his protruding ears and he smiled blissfully straight into the faces of the sun and Mrs Craggs.

The upper half of the window jammed and while Mrs Craggs tugged at the frame impatiently, furrowing her brows with increasing anger, a window on the left rattled and a high uneven little voice clucked:

'Good morning, Mrs Craggs. No, what do you think of that, eh? No, how do you like it? No, I'll run round to you now—no, I can't . . .'

Mrs Fitzgerald's attitude to the whole world was characterised by a minus sign: No. This minus had appeared when they had been forced to sell their castle in Scotland and move to Abbot Street. The minus pierced Bailey the organist like an arrow. And how could it be otherwise when one of Mrs Fitzgerald's nine daughters had long been running over to Bailey the organist for 'private lessons'?

Mrs Craggs went down into the marble dining-room and as always the same unchanging curtain of the lightest opaque silk was on her lips.

'Craggs, Mrs Fitzgerald's coming over now. Your trousers are hanging out upstairs. And by the way, that Bailey's becoming quite impossible, you know. He's forever gazing into the bedroom window.'

The little iron monument stood motionless on its pedestal

and only the blades of its eyes were visible from beneath the lowered eyelids.

'If he's forever at it, then why have you never . . . Still, I'll have a word with him today after church. Yes, I will!'

Mrs Craggs turned to let down the blinds. 'Yes, please do. And make sure he knows you mean it. The sun's so bright it's really quite painful, isn't it?'

Mrs Fitzgerald was already knocking at the door. Mrs Fitzgerald was a turkey. Her head was always to one side on her outstretched neck and one eye was always raised up to the sky—at any moment a kite might swoop down and steal one of her nine little chicks.

Mrs Fitzgerald clucked on about the organist, her voice rising and falling. 'No, just think. There isn't a single young, pretty girl in the parish who hasn't . . . who hasn't . . . No, his poor wife, she's simply an angel. She locks all the money away from him and hides the doorkey but he manages to get out through the window . . . And just now I glanced out of the window . . . No, just think.'

Mrs Fitzgerald directed one eye at the sky and the other at Mrs Craggs. Mrs Craggs entered the pause as though it were an open door, without knocking, 'I've just asked Craggs to talk to Mr Bailey about it. It will be most amusing. Come and see the show after church.'

With one eye Mrs Fitzgerald was still mistrustfully searching the sky for the kite, 'Oh, Mrs Craggs, I know that you aren't at all like the others. I know you're not.'

The little iron monument looked up at Mrs Craggs without moving and without lifting its eyelids. 'What is she like then?'

Who could tell? The cord of the curtain was lost.

4

Abbot Street was still London and yet no longer London. Here people knew their neighbours very well and of course everyone knew the esteemed Mr Craggs. Everyone knew that at the Stock Exchange, or wherever it was, Mr Craggs was successful in his deals. He had a current account at the London City and Midland Bank, a beautiful wife and was one of the voluntary apostles of the Society for the Fight against Vice. And so naturally Mr Craggs' procession in his new trousers to St George's church was a triumphant procession.

Honouring the pavement with every step, the shortened monument smacked its feet, fixing itself to one pedestal for a moment, then a second, then a third: the pavement was an integrated line of pedestals stretching from home to church. Without lifting its eyelids, the monument smiled graciously, its top hat flashing continually in the sun. It stepped out, graced by the company of Mrs Craggs. Just as the bas-reliefs on Richard the Lionheart's pedestal grace him discreetly, but fittingly.

And finally the equation that was Mr Craggs' triumphant procession worked itself out: he reached the church.

Windows—narrow abysses into the world. On the coloured panes: deer, shields, skulls and dragons. The glass was green below and above it was orange. The greenness crept along the floor in a soft, thick moss. Footsteps were muffled, and it grew more and more silent, silent as the depths. Who could tell where the rest of the world was: the crab, the cheek, the unstitched seam in the stocking, one-eyed Mrs Fitzgerald, the spoons in their boxes, thirty-two years . . .?

Up in the choir Bailey the organist began to play. Silently, slyly the orange sun grew above the green moss. And now it shone violently above, directly overhead and you could only breathe through your mouth, as in the tropics. Weeds entangled wildly, shaggy stems rose up convulsively to the sun. The orange-black branches of the bass voices, with a gentle gruffness, reached deeper and deeper inside, and there was no escape. Women opened up like shells and God was flung into the heat by their prayers. And perhaps only Mrs Laurie Craggs sat magnificent as always, made of marble.

'You haven't forgotten about Bailey?' whispered Mrs Craggs to her husband as the service was ending.

'Me, forget? Oh, no . . .' a blade flashed from under Mr Craggs' lowered eyelids.

One-eyed Mrs Fitzgerald anxiously looked up at the imaginary kite, gathered her nine little chicks in their white dresses under her wings and stood on her toes so as not to lose Mr Craggs in the crowd and miss the outcome of his meeting with Bailey. Outside by the church doors lay the tomb of a certain Haig, a knight beheaded at some time for his papist beliefs. On a stone, arrayed in stone armour, lay the headless knight. And by this knight who had lost his head, women were clustering around Bailey the organist.

'Mr Bailey, you played particularly well today. I prayed so hard, so hard that . . .'

'Mr Bailey, would you mind . . . I just wanted . . .'

'Mr Bailey, you know that you . . . that you . . .'

High above their open, expectant lips swayed the organist's head with his translucent ears, curling up at the edges. And higher still, squinting at its own brightness, the sun rushed headlong, without caring where it was going.

The organist had long arms like a monkey's, but even so he couldn't embrace them all at once. The organist shook his head blissfully.

'My dears, if only I could . . .'

Bailey the organist began to think about Isis with her thousand outstretched arms, with her thousand flowering nipples, with a womb like the earth, receiving all seed.

'Ah, my dear Bailey. Of course, he's surrounded as usual. Have you a minute?' It was Craggs. He rose up on to the last step, graced by the marble company of Mrs Craggs, and waited.

Bailey turned like the needle of a compass, pulled off his hat, and ran up, tripping over his own feet. He squeezed Mr Craggs' hand and his eyes shone at him. You could almost hear: Dearest Craggs, inimitable Craggs, you too, adorable Craggs . . .

The three of them moved to one side and only Mrs

Fitzgerald remained unobtrusively behind them, nodding her head approvingly at Craggs' every word and firing minus signs with one eye at Bailey's back like arrows.

'Listen, my dear Bailey. My wife has been telling me that you're constantly spoiling the view from her bedroom window. What have you got to say about it, eh?'

The sun's wine was ringing in Bailey's head and he couldn't hear the words clearly. But when he did hear them, Bailey was crushed. He frowned and a mass of loose skin immediately appeared on his face; he looked like a baggy suit, bought in a ready-to-wear shop.

'Mrs Craggs? It . . . it can't be . . .' Bailey's lips flapped in confusion. 'Mrs Craggs, you can't have told him. No, of course not, how could I even . . . not you. Of course not . . .'

It began to seem funny that he had believed it even for a second. He waved his hand and smiled blissfully.

Mrs Craggs raised her eyebrows. She hesitated. Craggs' claws were already stirring on his stomach. Mrs Fitzgerald stood on her toes looking pleased.

But at the very last moment Mrs Craggs loudly burst out laughing. 'Just imagine, Mr Bailey, I did say it. And you know that I was finally forced to say it. Yes, you know it very well.'

Bailey blinked. Again he was the baggy suit from the ready-to-wear shop. Suddenly, with both hands he pulled his hat over his eyes and, without saying goodbye, without listening to Craggs any further, he ran off along the asphalt, getting his feet tangled. Mrs Fitzgerald's minus signs streamed after him. He ran on and in midstep, for no reason at all, he stopped dead. Goodness knows what entered his head or what he remembered, but he smiled broadly, blissfully and waved his hat joyfully at the Craggs.

Craggs shrugged his shoulders. 'He's simply off his head.'

And he moved off homewards, from one pedestal to the next, from that to the third, along the endless line of pedestals.

5

The sun had driven London into a frenzy. London rushed onwards.

A torrent of top hats, of huge-brimmed white hats and impatiently open lips burst through the dam. The elephant buses sped along in a herd, in a fever from the spring. Lowering their heads, they sniffed each other like dogs. The street posters yelled out in raspberry, green and orange voices: 'Rolls-Royce', 'Waltz—the two of us', 'Automatic Sun'. And everywhere little boys in white collars ran quick as lightning between the flashing legs, letters and wheels with extra editions of the newspapers.

The top hats, the elephant buses, Rolls-Royce, Automatic Sun—all burst their banks and would of course have washed away the houses and the statues of policemen at the cross-roads, if there had not been an outlet down into the Underground and the subterranean lines of the 'Tube'. The lifts swallowed one helping after another and lowered them into the sweltering belly. Here, the frenzied blood pulsated and sped more frantically along the resounding concrete tubes.

In a frenzy, London poured out wildly beyond the town into parks, on to the grass. People hurried, drove, walked and pushed newly-born infants in innumerable wicker prams.

Mrs Craggs watched the procession of the innumerable prams along the asphalt through the transparent glass of the window. Mrs Fitzgerald knocked anxiously at the Craggs' window.

'Mrs Craggs! Listen, Mrs Craggs! Is my Annie with you? No? Well, that's that—she's dashed out of town again with that . . . No, Mrs Craggs, you're lucky, you haven't any children.'

On Mrs Craggs' marble brow there were two very fine, dark lines like veins. Perhaps they were only proof of the authenticity of the marble. Or perhaps they were the only cracks in that most immaculate marble.

'And where is Mr Craggs?' Mrs Fitzgerald glanced up apprehensively with one eye.

'Mr Craggs? He said he had to go somewhere in connection with that society of his, the Fight against Vice.'

'No, you're so lucky, so lucky . . .'

Mrs Craggs crossed the dining-room. The legs of one of the metal chairs had moved out of their designated hollows in the carpet. Mrs Craggs moved the chair. She went upstairs to the bedroom and lifted the blind. The window was open and the air in the bedroom grew fresh. Although Mrs Craggs was sure that the window was open, still for some reason she felt it necessary to raise the blind and check.

While Mrs Craggs settled down in the dining-room once more and observed the procession of innumerable prams, Mr Craggs—the small white cross of an apostle of the Fight against Vice in his lapel—was hurtling leisurely along the resounding tubes. His iron lids were lowered into an extra edition of the newspaper. At three o'clock zeppelins had been sighted over the North Sea. This was most opportune.

'Excellent. Excellent.' Mr Craggs foresaw success. The atmosphere was just right. Mr Craggs decided to make use of this atmosphere—on Hampstead Heath.

Hampstead Heath was full to the brim with champagne: a fine mist, golden with tiny sparks. Couples were sitting close together on benches, shoulder to shoulder, pressing nearer to each other. Their tiresome clothing turned to ashes. The sun's champagne streamed from one body into another. And there was a couple on the green silk of the grass, covered by a raspberry umbrella. Only their feet and a little bit of lace could be seen. In the magnificent universe beneath the raspberry umbrella, with closed eyes, they drank in the sparkling madness.

'Extra! Extra! Zeppelins over the North Sea at three o'clock.'

But under the umbrella, in the raspberry universe, they were immortal. What did it matter that in another far-away universe people would be killing each other?

A merry-go-round of lightning-quick boys rushed past:

collectors of cigarette ends, sellers of the extra editions, of happiness, kissing pigs, patented pills for men. A raucous Punch, machines on wheels pouring out smoke, selling sausages and chestnuts, and flocks of top hats walking in single file, like the elephant buses in a spring fever. There was a piercing, unbearable whistle, like a whiplash. Once more it lashed. Heads poked out from under the raspberry umbrella, the top hats and the huge white hats. A little iron monument was standing on a table, gravely blowing a whistle.

'Ladies and gentlemen.' Mr Craggs stopped whistling. 'Ladies and gentlemen, the extra edition reports that zeppelins have been sighted over the North Sea. Ladies and gentlemen, take a good look at yourselves. Are you ready to die? Death is coming today. It is you who will die . . . No, no, not your neighbour, but you yourself, delightful lady under the raspberry umbrella. You are smiling, your teeth are shining, but have you ever seen the smile of a skull? Stop—just for a moment—think hard. Have you done all you should before you die? You, under the raspberry umbrella!'

'Not yet! Not quite everything!' the Punch who up to now had been silent squeaked in a thin voice.

Everybody laughed. The delightful lady laughed and hid herself beneath the raspberry sky of the umbrella. It was obvious to everyone that she was pressing her knees against her Adam. They were alone in a raspberry universe and they were immortal. The park was brimming with tiny sparks.

Mr Craggs circled the raspberry universe. A pair of ladies' black shoes and a pair of men's brown shoes could be seen sticking out from under the umbrella. The men's brown shoes and the blue silk socks with brown spots were obviously of the best and most expensive kind. This was worth noticing.

Mr Craggs strolled on, carrying his huge crab claws in front of him on his stomach, with his eyelids lowered.

Mr Craggs ate his dinner with his eyelids lowered whilst

at the next table the delightful lady from beneath the raspberry umbrella was eating her dinner. She was bursting with the sweet amber juice of the sun. It was agonising how badly she needed somebody to drink up some of it. She was an apple on a windless, sultry evening, ripe, growing transparent, suffocating. Ah, if only it would break off the branch soon and fall to the earth. The apple-lady from beneath the raspberry umbrella got up and her Adam got up too. It did not matter who he was, he was just the earth. Slow and heavy, they walked up the hill which glowed lilac in the twilight, reached the top and slowly sank into the earth on the other side. Their heads were only a raspberry umbrella—then there was nothing.

Mr Craggs waited a minute. Still hiding something beneath his lowered eyelids, he climbed up the hill, looked around, and with the agility of a rat, unexpected in a monument, he scampered down.

Down below, everything was quickly becoming furred, everything was growing over with a violet evening coat: trees, people. Under the heavy fur coats of the bushes, gentle, hairy animals were breathing quickly and whispering. Mr Craggs, furry and inaudible, snuffled about the park like an enormous rat out of a dream. There was a flash of blades—the blades of his eyes on his furry snout. They had opened as night fell. Mr Craggs was panting. The raspberry umbrella was nowhere to be seen.

'A boat . . .' Mr Craggs' claws tightened and grasped this. Once or twice before he had made a catch in a boat.

A still pond, black as pitch. A pair of swans in the middle shone dazzlingly white in their nakedness. And in the distance a welcoming willow hung down over a boat. Mr Craggs slapped his feet more quickly along the grass. The swans grew, nearer and nearer, whiter and whiter. On tiptoe, he carefully leant over the trunk of the tree.

The boat lay below. At one end of it, hiding their faces, the soft furry umbrella was a dark circle, which a short while before had still been raspberry-coloured, and at the other end somebody's legs shone as white as swans in the darkness. Mr Craggs wiped his face with a handkerchief and unclenched his claws. Feeling pleased with himself, he lay resting for a minute. Then, furry and inaudible, he crawled down through the slippery mud on his stomach.

'Good evening, my friends.' A little monument rose up by the boat. Its eyelids were chastely lowered. Its protruding nose, jaw and lips smiled.

Something swan-white flashed and then vanished. There was a cry. The umbrella leapt into the water and floated away. A shaggy animal jumped out of the boat at Craggs.

'What the devil . . .? What . . . what right have you . . .? Just let me get my . . .'

Mr Craggs smiled, lowering his eyelids. The terrible crab claws unclenched and then tightened round the arms of the delightful apple-lady's Adam. And Adam, panting, had fallen into the trap. Mr Craggs smiled.

'You will have to come with me to the nearest police station, you and your young lady—I'm very sorry. There you'll have to give your names, both of you. And then we'll meet in court. I'm very sorry to have to say this to you. And tell your young lady to stop crying: the punishment for indecent behaviour in a public place isn't very heavy.'

'Listen here . . . Damn it! Will you let go of my arms! I'm telling you . . .'

But Mr Craggs held on tightly. The apple-lady was now on her knees on the sand, covering her face with her hands, pleading incoherently through her sobs. Mr Craggs smiled.

'I really am very sorry for you, my dear lady. You're still so young, and to appear in court . . .'

'Oh, ask anything you like but not that! Do you want . . .?' The lady's arms shone white as a swan in the darkness.

'Very well, then. But only for you, enchanting young lady. Promise that you will ne-ver again . . .'

'Oh, you're so . . . merciful . . . like a God. I promise you . . . Oh, yes, I promise.'

With one claw still holding the crushed and deflated Adam, Craggs took out his whistle and put it in his mouth. 'You see, one step and I'll blow on it . . .' and he let go of his captive. He looked him over from his silk socks up to his head, sizing him up, and said abruptly, 'Fifty guineas.'

'Fifty . . . guineas?' The man took a step towards Craggs. Craggs began to blow a shrill whistle. As yet it was barely audible, but at any moment . . . The captive stopped.

'Well? Have you your cheque book with you? I'll shine a light for you,' Mr Craggs suggested obligingly and took out a pocket torch.

The captive, gnashing his teeth, wrote out a cheque to the London City and Midland Bank. The lady floated after her umbrella with dumbfounded eyes. The umbrella slowly disappeared into the darkness, never to return. Mr Craggs, holding the whistle between his teeth, smiled: that was two months provided for. Fifty guineas! Mr Craggs was not often that lucky.

6

Darkness. The door into the neighbouring room is not quite shut. A strip of light stretches through the crack in the door, across the ceiling. People are walking about by lamplight. Something has happened. The strip moves faster and faster and the dark walls move further and further apart, into infinity. This room is London and there are thousands of doors. The lamps dart about and the strips dart across the ceiling. And perhaps it is all delirium . . .

Something had happened. The black sky above London burst into fragments: white triangles, squares and lines—the silent geometric delirium of searchlights. The blinded elephant buses rushed somewhere headlong with their lights extinguished. The distinct patter along the asphalt of belated couples, like a feverish pulse, died away. Everywhere doors slammed and lights were put out. And the city lay deserted, hollow, geometric, swept clean by a sudden plague: silent domes, pyramids, circles, arches, towers, battlements.

The silence swelled out for a moment, stretching like a soap bubble and then burst. Far away bombs began to whine and stamp with iron feet. Growing taller and taller, reaching up to the sky, a delirious truncated creature—just legs and belly—stupidly and blindly stamped the bombs on to the ants and their square anthills below. Zeppelins . . .

The lifts did not have time to swallow them all. The ants poured down the emergency stairs. They clung on to the footboards and then with a roar sped along the tubes, without caring where they were going and got off without caring where they were. They crowded together in the delirious underground world with its concrete sky hanging over them, its confusion of caves, staircases, suns, kiosks, vending machines.

'Zeppelins over London! Extra! Extra!' The mechanical, clockwork boys scurried about.

Mr Craggs was speeding along standing in a carriage, holding on to a strap and did not lift his eyes from the extra edition of the newspaper. The top hats and the huge white hats were continually increasing, pushing him off his pedestal, against somebody's knees. The knees trembled. Mr Craggs glanced down and saw the apple-lady.

'Ah, what's this? You're here too? Delighted . . . I do beg your pardon: it's so crowded.' Mr Craggs took off his hat with a smile.

The apple-lady was alone. She answered Mr Craggs with a blank, submissive smile. In Craggs' inside left pocket lay the cheque for fifty guineas and it warmed his heart.

Mr Craggs joked politely, 'We're like the early Christians, obliged to take refuge in the catacombs. It's most amusing, don't you think, Miss?'

Miss ought to have laughed, but could not. She tried with all her might and finally did burst out laughing. Something absurd and indecently loud came out, filling the carriage. Everyone turned round. Mr Craggs, lifting his top hat, hurriedly moved on.

'Hammersmith! Train terminates here.' The conductor rattled the door and everyone poured out of the carriage.

A muffled, iron rumble could be heard coming down the liftshafts and staircases. The top hats and huge white hats worn to one side remained on the platform. They clung to the blindingly white walls and merged with the raspberry and green posters, with the faces speeding motionlessly in the Rolls-Royce car, with the Automatic Sun. In the white, tiled catacombs a crowd of strange Christians out of posters were taking refuge.

The apple-lady looked around, feeling lost. Her eyes lighted on the one familiar figure, with his claws folded across his stomach and his flapping feet. Mechanically, as if in a dream, she entered a lift together with Craggs. The lift took them on to the streets. There, white triangles and lines flashed against the black sky. The silent tortoise houses and trees hurried along, pattering and rumbling. The apple-lady caught up with Craggs.

'Excuse me . . . I'm sorry . . . Could you possibly take me somewhere . . . I was supposed to be going to Leicester Square. I don't understand what's going on.'

The little iron monument stopped still for a moment—for ages. From beneath his lowered eyelids, the blade of an eye shone in the darkness.

'I'm really very sorry, but I'm hurrying home. And besides . . .' Mr Craggs laughed silently. It was utterly absurd to think of him and some . . .

An enormous hornet droned directly overhead in the tightly stretched silence. Mr Craggs hurried on. Laurie was alone. He slapped his feet rapidly along the asphalt. He thought the cheque had stopped rustling in his pocket. He drew to a halt to feel for it and heard tiny, tremulous footsteps behind him. A shadow was running towards him from afar, like a lost dog without its master, timid and cowed.

It was clear that this . . . this woman would follow him right up to his door, would stand there all night, would sit on the steps and do something altogether ridiculous, the sort of thing that happens in a dream. Mr Craggs wiped his forehead with a handkerchief and, looking over his shoulder, flitted into the nearest dark alleyway so as to get home through the yard. Mr Craggs found his gate by feeling along until he came to the edges of the bricks by the gate post and then knocked. In the dark window of the bedroom a face shone dimly white. It was clearly Mrs Craggs' face. Mrs Craggs swung her arm and threw something out of the window. What could this mean? Mr Craggs knocked for a long time, louder and louder, until the whole of Abbot Street could hear, but the gate did not open. Mr Craggs considered the position and tried to think of some explanation, when suddenly, very close to him, the iron feet stamped. Fragments of glass tinkled, Mr Craggs' top hat fell off, and as he caught it, the little monument fell down on to the asphalt.

7

On Sundays, when Mr Craggs was not at home, Mrs Craggs entertained her mother and sister. They came from Whitechapel at dusk, knocked gingerly at the back gate and came into the dining-room through the kitchen. They sat on the very edge of their chairs in the metallic dining-room, drank their tea wearing their hats and ate one piece of cake each.

'But, please, my dears, do have some more. There's another just the same, a whole one, in the sideboard.' Mrs Craggs opened the sideboard ceremoniously.

'No, thank you. Really . . .' The guests licked their lips and, sitting on the very edge of their chairs, they kept an ear open so as not to miss the familiar slapping of feet and be able to vanish in time into the kitchen. But all that could be heard was the creak of the innumerable wicker prams along the asphalt.

'You are so lucky, Laurie,' sighed the guests in admiration. 'Do you remember how you used to come to the market with us . . . And now . . .'

The marble blushed: it was so necessary to receive outside confirmation of one's good fortune.

The three of them went into the bedroom. Mrs Craggs turned on the light, its crystal pendants sparkled, their eyes shone. On the bed, on the chairs lay the unbelievable laciness, the delicate whiteness and the spiderweb.

'Do, please, Laurie. You must look just like a queen in white.'

Mrs Craggs undressed behind a screen. She came out dressed in black stockings and slippers and something of the finest white. Mrs Craggs' warm marble glowed barely pink through the whiteness. The crystal pendants played in the light, glowing pink, and the pink curtain fluttered more quickly on Mrs Craggs' lips, about to be lifted by the wind.

'You are so lucky, Laurie,' the guests sighed in admiration.

Downstairs somebody was knocking at the door. All three had one thought: Craggs.

'Good heavens! It's already dark. We should have gone home long ago.' The guests leapt up.

Mrs Craggs hurriedly threw on her white dressing gown, led her mother and sister out through the back, and then opened the front door. But it was not Craggs. A little boy in a white collar stood in the doorway with a package. He sniffed innocently, but one mousey eye winked slyly.

'For you, madam.' He handed over the package. In the package, as last Sunday, was a bouquet of tea roses, with petals that stuck out and curled up at the edges.

Mrs Craggs flared up. 'Return them.' She thrust the bouquet angrily back at the boy.

The boy winked even harder. 'Where to? The shop won't take them back. They've been paid for.'

Mrs Craggs ran to the bedroom with the bouquet. The roses were fading and the petals scattered down the staircase. Mrs Craggs looked around in confusion. She shoved the bouquet under the heap of lace on the chair and went downstairs, picking up the petals from the steps on her way.

She held out threepence to the little boy, trying to look up beyond the knowing wink of the mousey eye. There, up above her, was the black mosaic of the sky, made of creeping white triangles and squares.

'Oh, yes, of course, that's the zeppelins going over,' said the little boy cheerfully in answer to her raised eyebrows. 'It'll start any minute now. Thank you, madam.' And he plunged into the darkness.

Mrs Craggs lowered the blinds in the dining-room and, shining like metal, put away the celebrated spoons, each in its correct box. She had to be quick, before it all started. At the sixth spoon, decorated with three castles, the arms of Newcastle, there was a muffled explosion. The spoon with the three castles remained on the table, next to the empty box. With a rumble, dull, iron feet stamped on the houses and the people, getting nearer and nearer. Another step and Mrs Craggs' world would be destroyed: Craggs, the spoons, the unbelievable laciness.

There were five minutes left to live. She must do the most important thing.

'The bouquet . . . The most important thing is to get rid of the bouquet,' Mrs Craggs said to herself in a great hurry. In her bedroom she snatched the bouquet from under the heap of lace.

'Yes, into the yard. I'll throw it to him in the yard so that he . . .' She leant out of the window and swung her arm. The delirious, geometric sky swept past, now very close, and in the yard next door, stood a black, swaying cardboard cut-out. Mrs Craggs angrily threw the bouquet right into its face and heard—perhaps she was delirious—the funniest, childish sobbing.

Close by, an ironfoot stamped. Fragments of glass tinkled. Everything was falling and Mrs Craggs' world collapsed: the spoons, the lace.

'Bailey! Bailey!' The ruined Mrs Craggs flew headlong down the stairs into the yard.

The delirious sky flashed momentarily. An absurdly thin black figure flashed against the wall. And the tender lips, like a foal's, drew apart the curtain across Mrs Craggs's lips. There was only a minute left to live.

On the asphalt, strewn with coal dust, they lived for a minute—for an age in an immortal raspberry universe. Someone was knocking endlessly at the gate. But in the faraway raspberry universe they did not hear anything.

The electric lights were out. For a long time Mr Craggs wandered through the rooms, his feet faltering in the furry darkness, crushing fragments of glass, calling out, 'Laurie! Where are you, Laurie?'

The reverberating iron footsteps moved off southwards and grew fainter.

At last Mr Craggs found a candle and ran upstairs into the bedroom. And in the doorway, right behind him, appeared Mrs Craggs.

'Good Lord! Where have you been?' Mr Craggs turned on his pedestal. 'My top hat . . . Do you realise, it knocked off my top hat . . .' Mr Craggs lifted the candle and his mouth fell open: Mrs Craggs' white dressing gown was undone and the delicate white material underneath was torn and covered in coal dust. There were tears on her lashes, and her lips . . .

There was no curtain.

'What's happened to you? You're not hurt, Laurie?'

'Yes . . . I mean, no. Oh, no!' Mrs Craggs laughed. 'I've just . . . Go out for a moment. I'll change now and come down to the dining-room. It seems it's all over.'

Mrs Craggs changed, carefully picked up the petals from the floor, put them into an envelope and put the envelope into a box. Somewhere in the south the iron footsteps died away. It was all over.